Legends of
The Mountain State 3

For Bella Grace

Legends of the Mountain State 3

More Ghostly Tales from the State of West Virginia

Editor Michael Knost

Woodland Press, LLC

CHAPMANVILLE, WEST VIRGINIA

Copyright © 2009 Woodland Press

ISBN 978-0-9824939-2-2

All rights reserved. Written permission must be secured from Woodland Press, LLC to use or reproduce any part of this book in any form or by any means—graphic, electronic, or mechanical, including photocopying, recording, taping, or by any information storage retrieval system—except for brief quotations in reviews or articles.

SAN: 254-9999

FOREWORD

West Virginians love good stories. They like to tell them and they like to hear them, even if they're stories that scare them half to death. I grew up in the little mining town of Coalwood down in McDowell County and, let me tell you, it was a place filled with ghost stories, and we kids got told more than a few of them. It's a wonder my hair didn't turn as white back then as it is now. One of the first stories I recall was when the old mine was still active and train tracks went through town. All night, the train rumbled past our house, the wheels of the loaded coal cars screeching like banshees and the locomotive holding forth with its terrible whistle as literally thousands of tons of steel and coal hurtled past us only a few yards away.

One night after I'd gone to bed, the train whistle blew and kept blowing, and the coal cars began to screech especially loud, so loud it was like they were in the same room. I thought maybe the end of the world was at hand. I heard my folks get up and then Mom threw open the door of the room where my brother and I slept and ordered us to stay inside. The next morning, I found out why. A miner on his way to work on the hootowl shift had gotten run over by the train. He was a miner my dad had recently hired so folks didn't know much about him except that he'd not only been run over, he'd gotten his head cut off. The older kids at school had an awful lot to say about that, and the way they told it was all pretty scary. They led us to the place on the tracks where the terrible thing had actually happened and talked about how that miner's head had just rolled and rolled down the tracks, the train knocking it along until it had been pushed clear out of Coalwood, probably all the way to Bradshaw as far as anybody knew. That was bad enough, imagining a head being rolled all the way to Bradshaw, but then the stories started about a ghostly apparition walking the track at night. It was headless, of course, and everybody assumed it was that miner looking for his head or any head he could get. Yes, I know it was like that story Washington Irving told about the headless horseman in Sleepy Hollow, but this was no legend concocted by some Yankee way up north. This was Coalwood, deep in the misty hollows of West Virginia, where anything could happen, including an upset dead coal miner who'd be happy to steal your head to replace his own. I can tell you I was never more relieved when the coal company decided to take out those train tracks and shift their operations over on the other side of the mountain. I hoped that poor miner's ghost would shift his operations over there, too. I guess he did, at least for a while. The last time I was in Coalwood, somebody told me he was back. Maybe that's why I left town at sundown, I don't know.

Of course, the headless miner was just one scary story of many, including the tale of a type of giant West Virginia bird that enjoyed picking up dead tree limbs in their beaks and beating them on hollow tree stumps. Why these birds liked to do that was never explained. What was explained, however, was that they also liked to swoop down on little boys, clutch them in their sharp claws, and carry them away to feed to their chicks. One time, a miner with a chaw in his cheek and an expression of complete honesty on his coal-blackened face told us if we wanted to see one of these terrible birds, all we had to do was go up on that mountain (he pointed which one) because he himself that very morning had seen one up there. He cautioned us, however, that we'd better be prepared to run like lightning else that awful bird, which he called a whoppercod, would get us. Laughing at the foolishness of the miner's story, we climbed up the designated mountain and blamed if we didn't hear a thumping sound that seemed to be getting closer. I want to tell you we couldn't get off that mountain fast enough! Was it real? Well, if that miner was making the story of the whoppercod up, what was that noise which sounded an awful lot like a big stick whomping on a hollow stump? Answer me that!

Sometimes, the stories were a little silly but still effective. I recall one evening, my gang was following some big kids around and generally making a nuisance out of ourselves when they told us a midget had escaped from the circus and was on its way to Coalwood to eat little boys. We had no idea what a midget was (I guessed it was some sort of big lizard), but I can tell you we all went home and stayed there for the rest of the night, which, come to think of it, might have been the plan, I don't know.

Anyway, there was probably no better (or worse) scary storyteller than Red Carroll who was O'Dell Carroll's dad. O'Dell was one of those famous Rocket Boys I wrote about in the book by the same name and was in that movie titled *October Sky*. If you were unlucky enough to find yourself in Red's presence, he'd likely lay one of his stories on you, stories of dead people that rose from the grave and were stalking around Coalwood, *maybe right at that very moment*. One time, Roy Lee Cooke, another Rocket Boy, and I found ourselves at O'Dell's house after dark and Red began to hold forth on a story so scary that I won't let myself recall it, even now. There was a long stretch of unlit road between O'Dell's house and the part of Coalwood where Roy Lee and I lived, and we didn't get more than a few yards down it before we came running back, begging for Red to take us home in his car. To this day, Red laughs about how scared Roy Lee and I were that night and that's OK with me as long as he doesn't tell that story again. I'm not sure my heart could take it.

I guess the writers in this book are a lot like Red Carroll and the other Coalwood storytellers. They know how to tell a good tale, and they don't mind scaring us, more than a little. So sit back and enjoy, or cringe, or whatever you do when you read or hear a scary story. And if you are away from home and get too scared, I guess you can call Red Carroll over in Coalwood. Maybe he'll come drive you to your house like he did me and Roy Lee. But, whatever you do, don't let him tell you one of his stories on the way.

Trust me on this.

Homer Hickam

INTRODUCTION

While attending book signings and events throughout the great state of West Virginia, I enjoy hearing folks talk about the *Legends of the Mountain State* series. I can't help but swell with pride each time someone tells me they can't wait for the *next* edition to come out so they can devour it as quickly as they'd devoured its predecessors.

Sure, it's nice to hear praise from famous writers, politicians, and publishing professionals, but nothing compares to the knowledge that West Virginia readers enjoy this series. It makes me proud to know the state's residents approve of the stories and the projects, which uses the Mountain State as the beautiful backdrop to make these tales come alive.

Our state is often portrayed with absurd stereotypical elements. Movies like *Deliverance*, *Wrong Turn*, and many others offer the impression that the Mountain State is overflowing with ignorant, incestuous, bloodthirsty hillbillies—and as my fellow Mountaineers know, that simply is a false view.

This is why I love the *Legends of the Mountain State* series. Writers from all over the United States (and a few from Canada) offer respectful stories depicting our citizens as normal American's caught in the middle of a spooky legend or ghost story.

But after three volumes of legends and ghostly tales, this will be the last edition in the series. We feel the time has come for us to look at other projects, many of which may be somewhat similar in nature. For those who have devoured the stories, I want to say thank you for supporting these endeavors. For those who have read only one book, I suggest you read the others, as you will see that each has its own fingerprint and DNA as it pertains to storytelling, varying legends, as well as style, tone, and voice.

Now, go make sure all the doors are all locked. Check the windows that they are closed and latched. And for heaven's sake, turn all the lights on in your house before you begin reading.

Wait. Did you just hear a noise?

Michael Knost

TABLE OF CONTENTS

The Caretaker
Elizabeth Massie .... Page 1

Flowers In Winter
Michael West .... Page 11

Wampus Cat
Scott Nicholson .... Page 21

George's Head
John R. Little .... Page 37

A Banshee in Beckley
Brian J. Hatcher .... Page 43

Calling the Dead
Kelli Dunlap .... Page 53

Richard Dawson and the Family Feud Phantasms
Matt Venne .... Page 63

Her Father's Collection
Douglas F. Warrick .... Page 75

Where You Gonna Run To
Steve Vernon .... Page 85

The Rose Ghost of Ravenswood
Fran Friel .... Page 95

Springs Eternal
Matthew Warner .... Page 103

The Angry Dark
Mark Justice .... Page 111

Trapped
J.G. Faherty .... Page 123

Other Great Book Titles From Woodland Press, LLC

Legends of the Mountain State
Ghostly Tales from the State of West Virginia
Edited by Michael Knost

Legends of the Mountain State 2
More Ghostly Tales from the State of West Virginia
Edited by Michael Knost

Writers Workshop of Horror
Edited by Michael Knost

The Secret Life and Brutal Death of Mamie Thurman
By F. Keith Davis

West Virginia Tough Boys
By F. Keith Davis

The Tale of the Devil
By Dr. Coleman C. Hatfield and Robert Spence

The Feuding Hatfields & McCoys
By Dr. Coleman C. Hatfield and F. Keith Davis

ARCH: The Life of Governor Arch A. Moore, Jr.
By Brad Crouser

Elizabeth Massie
THE CARETAKER

ELIZABETH MASSIE is a two-time Bram Stoker Award winning author of horror novels, media tie-ins, and short fiction. Her most recent novel is *DD Murphry, Secret Policeman* (October 2009) which she co-authored with Alan M. Clark. Beth lives in the Shenandoah Valley of Virginia with illustrator Cortney Skinner.

(Inspired by the murder of a preacher's wife by her husband in Cabin Thirteen at Babcock State Park, WV)

This lush, mountainous state park is my responsibility. I check the hiking trails to make sure they aren't strewn with broken glass or blocked by downed tree limbs. I take stock of the narrow wooden staircases that lead from the main road down to the creek-side cabins to see that they are solid and secure. I investigate the cabins to be certain no vandals have painted graffiti on them. I scan the brisk-running Glade Creek, watching for litter that might have been tossed there by careless sightseers. I've been doing this for a very long time, so long that my memory eludes me at times and no one pays me any attention. But I enjoy my work. It's steady, peaceful. And important.

The park is beautiful—each and every season. The spring blooms with dogwoods and redbuds and the songs of mockingbirds and robins.

The summer is bright with sunshine that shimmers on the oak leaves and sends hummingbirds to hover over Glade Creek. Autumn is alive with oranges and reds, crisp breezes through the gaps and hollows, and small creatures seeking food to store for the coming cold months.

But I especially enjoy the dead of winter—the silvered frost and swirling flakes, ice-blue skies and peaks blanketed in white. A smattering of visitors come to see the historic old creek-side mill, but for the most part, the park remains void of people. It has a different sound in the cold months; it is quieter, gentler, more mysterious. Yet still, I do my job. I stroll the frozen paths and trails, the staircases, the creek bank, the small yards in which the log cabins sit awaiting the turn of time and the arrival of lodgers once more.

It is December 31st, the eve of a new year. Snow fell throughout the night and all of the morning, leaving a deep, powdery shroud upon the rocks and ridges, treetops and river rocks. The late afternoon is bitterly cold.

No one is at the park today—no cars in the visitor's parking lot, no bundled and determined hikers, no photo bugs in hoods and gloves snapping quick shots of the mill before hopping back into their warm vehicles. They're all home with their loved ones, drinks and noisemakers in hand, preparing to sing "Auld Lang Syne" once the clock strikes midnight.

I stroll along the main road, listening to the rushing of the creek nearby. It's time for me to check the cabins. Crows spin overhead, calling to each other: "Uh oh. Uh oh." A coyote trots across the road in front of me, nose to the ground. Its fur stands on end as it becomes vaguely aware of my presence, but it continues on. Clearly, it knows I am no threat.

I take the wooden stairs down the snow-crusted embankment to cabin Number One. It is quiet, dark, and unvandalized. I climb back up then move along the road a bit farther to the steps that lead to cabin Number Two. I descend. The stairs are safe. The cabin is secure. The same is true for the other cabins, Three through Twelve.

But something is amiss at cabin Number Thirteen. I know it the moment I put my foot on the top step and peer down to the little clearing in which the cabin sits. My heart catches and my mouth goes dry. The cabin looks the same as the others—dark logs chinked with white mortar. A sloping roof, a front porch, several small windows that reflect the white of the world outside. A small yard surrounded by gangly saplings and leaf-bare trees. A lopsided picnic table at a tilt, one of its legs sinking in the soft ground where moles have dug tunnels.

I hear her crying.

It is a woman's voice, muffled inside Cabin Thirteen. A rush of fear courses through me, followed by a surge of compassion. No one should be staying here this time of year. The park is closed to lodgers. The cabins are all locked up tightly. And yet I hear her as sure as I hear the crows. I know the sound of pain and sorrow. I've dealt with quite a bit in my time.

As a young man in the 1930s, I experienced the hopelessness of the time, the anxiety of a country in a great depression. I saw women lose their minds and men take their own lives, unable to come to terms with the losses of their jobs, homes, and sense of self-worth. I saw vital souls reduced to despondent shadows.

Determined to help my own struggling family, I joined the Civilian Conservation Corp in 1933 along with many other young American men. Some of us were sent here, to West Virginia, to establish Babcock State Park. We constructed roads, bridges, and log buildings among the tree-covered slopes and deep ravines. We landscaped, paved, and planted. We created a get-away in the mountains where vacationers could enjoy nature and, perhaps, forget their troubles.

During my tour of duty with the CCC, I became a leader to the other men. At twenty-five, I was a few years older than the rest. They looked up to me. They listened to my advice when they were angry and came to me for encouragement when they were homesick. I cheered them and counseled them. The boys needed me as much as they needed their monthly paychecks. They called me Papa Frank. I took the honor seriously. Though I was physically strong, my greatest strength seemed to be in comforting, encouraging, and supporting the boys, and then wishing them well when it was time for them to go home.

I move down the wooden staircase and go around to the front to Cabin Thirteen. The porch looks like a giant, hooded eye, staring blankly into space. I can hear the rush of Glade Creek beyond the trees. Crows on the cabin roof stretch their glossy black wings and call out.

"Uh oh. Uh oh. Uh oh."

The crying inside the cabin is a bit louder now.

Taking a cold breath, I step onto the porch and enter the cabin. I'm surprised the door opens so easily. It was supposed to be locked.

Like all the others, this cabin consists of just two rooms. The front room serves as kitchen, living room, and bedroom. There is a rugged table by the front window, flanked by two chairs. A deck of playing cards is splayed out on the table, some face up, some face down. A double bed holds against the right wall, unmade. In the back wall is a stone fireplace, filled with cold, black ash. There is also a sink, refrigerator, and stove. Beside the stove is a low doorway that opens to the bathroom.

There is no one in the room.

And there is blood on the bed.

"Uh oh," call the crows from outside.

I stare at the blood. There is quite a bit of it pooled on the mattress. I step closer even though I don't want to. I peer over the side of the bed and see more blood on the floor beside the wall.

Then I hear her crying again, close, right behind me. Startled, I spin about to find her standing in the middle of the room. She is dressed in a white cotton nightgown and her hair is uncombed. Her eyes are wide and there is blood on the side of her head. She holds out one trembling hand in my direction. Her face is surreally pale.

"Who are you?" I ask gently, trying not to frighten her.

She sobs but does not answer.

I repeat, "Who are you?"

Her voice is barely audible. "Cheryl."

"What happened to you, Cheryl?"

"It was awful." Several tears slide down her face. They glisten like quicksilver.

"Tell me."

"We were playing cards. He and I were, and I was losing. But I didn't mind. I don't care much for cards." She shrugs vaguely, her shoulders rising, falling.

"And?"

"And then. . . then he said it was time for bed. I put on my gown and climbed into bed. He went into the bathroom and I closed my eyes, waiting for him to finish with his washing. But then. . ." She shivers violently as if a frigid wind has passed through her. "Then I heard him grunt, and I opened my eyes in time to see him swing a heavy piece of firewood down at my head."

I look at the injury. It's grave. "We need to get you to a doctor."

"I knew he didn't love me anymore," she says, looking past me to the bed. She reaches up to touch the wound and her hand appears translucent, shimmering. I can see the outline of her face through the hand. How bizarre. Perhaps I'm overtired and am imagining things.

"He wanted to be rid of me," she continues. "But why did he have to do this to me? Why didn't he just leave me? Was it the insurance? Was I more valuable dead than alive?"

I take a step closer to Cheryl. "You'll die if we don't get you medical attention immediately."

"He was a preacher, and yet he wanted me dead," she says, her eyes focusing back on me. Her eyes have an odd glow to them, like tiny twin furnaces, and I'm frightened. Still, she needs me.

"Please, let me help get you to a hospital."

She cocks her head slightly, and her brows furrow. "Why do you say that? You know I'm already dead."

I freeze in place. "What did you say?"

She shakes her head sadly; the movement leaves an iridescent trail that fades momentarily. "You've come to help me move on."

"I don't know what. . ." I begin.

"But you do know," she says. "My spirit has been waiting. Now, you've come to help me go home."

I open my mouth to speak but then shut it again. I don't know what to say. I stare at Cheryl as she walks to the window. She leans her hands on the windowsill and sighs, but no mist of breath fogs the pane. I can see a faint reflection of her face in the glass, but I can also see the snow on the yard through her body. The cold winter sun is setting now, and its dim light passes through her and collects on the floor.

Slowly I move to the window. I catch a glimpse of my own reflection in the glass next to hers. My face is young, angular, handsome, with dark hair and dark eyes. I blink, startled, that I should look like this. It has been a very long time since I was a youth with the CCC, a very long time since I've been tending the wilderness park. How can I still look this way? I should be a very, very old man.

But I'm not.

What is happening?

Cheryl slips her nearly transparent hand into mine and gives it a squeeze.

And it is her tentative, hopeful touch that lets me remember.

It was 1934. I was on my second tour with the CCC, still laying roads, mapping trails, and sending money to my parents. Benjamin Harper and I were on a particularly steep slope, cutting down trees to place along the trail for erosion control. Ben's axe slipped and struck me across the chest. I fell, gasping my heart, feeling the life flow out between my fingers. Ben fell beside me and wept, "Papa Frank! Oh, my God, no, don't die! I'll get help! Please hold on!"

But I couldn't hold on. And though he got help, I did die.

My body was taken back to my hometown and buried, but I remained here. My work was not finished.

I remember now.

Though I wander the park day after day after day, night after night after night, unnoticed by hikers and lodgers and rangers, making sure all is safe, my main responsibility is to those who die in the park. Each New Year's Eve, the spirits of all who lost their lives during the year come to me for encouragement, support, and help getting home.

"Papa Frank," whispers Cheryl. "Please help me go home. I've been here since April. I hate the memories of my husband and his betrayal. I don't want to suffer anymore. He has his own journey, and I have mine. I want this to be over."

I nod, then take her arm and escort her out of the cabin. I think back on the fact that I didn't have to unlock the cabin door to come in and I don't have to unlatch it to go out. That's not what ghosts do. We just go where we will upon this plane, unhindered by physical things.

We move off the porch into the snowy yard. The sun has set and the sky above the trees is pewter gray. Silvery, early-evening stars wink down upon us. Standing in the yard of Cabin Thirteen is an old man who had a heart attack while overlooking the creek back in March. There is a hiker who fell in September and broke his neck in a ravine. They both nod at me knowingly and appreciatively. Gathered around their feet are squirrels, chipmunks, rabbits, and foxes, blue jays, crows, and cardinals. There is a gray-muzzled hound dog who took his last glorious romp in the park with his master and whose old body just gave out. Little creatures that died throughout the year and now need my help so their spirits can go to their new home beyond this earth. Their bright eyes look at me expectantly.

I remember now. This is my job. It is an honor and I take it seriously. I tell them everything will be all right. I offer them encouragement and support. Soon they will be at peace. Then I raise my hands and bless them all on their way. And one by one, they nod, fade away, and wink out. Cheryl is last. She is the first murder victim I've helped, and I hope she will be the last. She smiles and puts her hand to her heart as she disappears.

Clouds move in over the stars, heralding another imminent snowfall. I stand alone in the yard of Cabin Thirteen and stare upward until the first flakes begin to swirl down on the breeze. It is near midnight. A new year will begin soon. I know I will forget all this, as I have year after year after year. Then next December 31st it will come back to me. I'll recall my most important purpose and do my job.

After a long while, I climb back up the steps leading to the road. Below me, below the cabin, the creek rushes on and on. Snow dances in the air before me. Tree branches shudder and moan. And I wonder.

When can I go home?

When can I join the others?

I sigh with a touch of momentary sadness. My breath does not cloud the air.

Michael West *TRUE*
FLOWERS IN WINTER

MICHAEL WEST is a member of the Horror Writers Association and served as President of its local chapter, Indiana Horror Writers. He lives and works in the Indianapolis area with his wife, their two children, their bird, Rodan, and turtle, Gamera. His children are convinced that spirits move through the woods near their home.

We will *be together.*

The declaration filled Derek's inner ear; a stranger's voice, but he felt its passion as if it were his own. He glanced up Church Street, found red brick silhouetted against gray sky. Shuttered windows peered at him between naked branches. A temporary hospital during the Civil War, the old North house currently served as a historical museum, and though Derek knew exactly how many bricks formed its two-story façade, this was the first time he'd actually laid eyes upon it.

He stood there in the snow, hypnotized, shivering, his desert camouflage making him conspicuous. Beneath his coat, he clutched a bouquet of red roses to his chest, protected their delicate petals from bitter winds. He'd been compelled to buy them, to bring them. He didn't know why, just as he didn't know whose voice echoed through his skull.

I will come to Lewisburg, it promised, and then, over and over again, *I will come for you.*

Soon, the compulsion to enter the house became too strong for Derek to resist. He made his way up the shoveled walkway, lines of wind-blown snow slithering across his path. The front steps were dark and speckled with rock salt.

Inside, warmth enveloped Derek, a lover welcoming him home. The visions that haunted him, however, had been those of an outsider. He stomped his feet on the mat and his eyes darted to and fro, taking in his new surroundings.

In the center of the room, postcards filled wire-framed towers. Off to the left, gas logs blazed in a stone fireplace. Two turn-of-the-century portraits hung above the mantle—a man and a woman. Brass nameplates dubbed them Melville and Claudia Bartlett.

A woman stood behind an antique cash register on the far right—her raven hair pulled back, her pale brow furrowed like drifted snow. She counted boxes of taffy, adjusting her inventory accordingly. "We're closing up for the night," she told him, and barely lifted her head from her bookkeeping. "It's almost four and—"

She froze, held him in a stunned, oblique stare.

Looking into her dark eyes, Derek was struck by a sense of déjà vu, the same feeling he had upon sighting this house for the first time. He glanced down and saw that he held the roses out. He quickly lowered the bouquet, his cheeks warm and red as the petals in his hand.

On the battlefield, he had stood his ground in the midst of explosions and sniper fire. But now, in this house, with this intimate stranger, he had a sudden urge to run and forget this madness. He was about to give in when the woman spoke up again, and what she said only added to the mystery.

"After all these years, you've finally come back."

His eyes widened; when he found his voice, it was far too meek for his liking. "You've seen me before?"

"Well, not *you*, no, but. . ." Her lips blossomed into an odd grin. "Oh, come on. A soldier. . . here. . . delivering flowers? Did someone put you up to this?"

"I don't know anyone in Lewisburg. I don't even know why I'm here. I just felt this urge to. . . to. . ." He stood there a moment, wanting to share, *needing* to share, but he did not care for the skeptical look this woman gave him. He did not care for it at all.

She'll think I'm crazy, trying for a Section 8. Who knows, maybe I am.

"Sorry to have bothered you." Derek marched over to the counter, dropped the roses in front of her, then turned away. "Have a nice evening."

"Now, hold on. Wait a minute."

When he looked back at her, her eyes were downcast, studying his flowers.

"It's not every day a man brings me roses." She brushed the soft petals with her fingers. "You can at least tell me your name."

"Derek. Derek Patterson."

"You really don't know the story, Derek?" She lifted her gaze to him, and it was like something remembered from a dream. "The girl, the soldier. . . none of it?"

"No."

"If you don't have to run off, I could tell you, give you a quick tour of the house."

"I'd hate to make you go through any trouble, ma'am."

She grinned. "It's Ginny. And it's no trouble."

"Then I think I'd like to hear it," he told her.

I think I need to hear it.

Ginny moved out from behind the counter. She wore a black skirt that came down to her ankles and high-heeled boots with silver buckles. "This way."

Derek followed her to a spectacular staircase, admiring the elaborate, hand-carved woodwork. He glanced up at the second floor. It was quite dark. "You mentioned a girl and a soldier?"

"They fell in love," Ginny told him as they mounted the stairs. "Of course, her parents didn't approve. I guess it would be a pretty boring legend if everyone was happy."

She laughed, a shaky giggle that betrayed her nervousness. Was it being alone here with him, Derek wondered, or something else?

"On tours," Ginny resumed, "I like to call the girl Abigail." She took each step slowly, cautiously, the aged wood creaking beneath her feet. "Her parents shipped her off, and she came here to live with her Aunt Claudia and Uncle Melville. They were very strict, especially Melville. He kept Abby locked away. The poor girl, she just laid up there on her bed and cried."

Ginny paused a moment, stared up into the gloom, perhaps realizing that she forgot to turn on the lamps, perhaps not. It almost looked as if she was trying to regain her courage, but that was probably Derek's imagination.

"Then it was Christmas," she said, finally taking the next step, "and they allowed Abby to return home to her parents for the holidays. And wouldn't you know it, her soldier, her true love, was waiting for her."

It was easy for Derek to imagine their tender reunion. How many times had he watched long-absent warriors embrace the joyous wives and girlfriends they left behind? Derek could not help but envy them. At the end of the day, he was alone but for the voice of a stranger.

They will never keep us apart.

Ginny clung to the wooden handrail as if it were all that separated her from the mouth of a very deep well. She went on with her story, her words echoing through the empty foyer. "The soldier—I like to call him John—vowed to follow his love to Lewisburg, promised to take her away from this house, this prison."

They reached the upper level. Outside, the wind howled and the walls groaned against its forceful push: a century-old stalemate. At either end of the hall, the windows glowed—streetlamps reflecting off the snow, casting bizarre shadows.

Ginny moved to a door on the opposite side of the hallway. She placed her hand on the knob and glanced back at Derek, her eyes sparkling in the dimness. "This was Abby's room."

The door opened with a squeal, short but shrill, and Derek followed Ginny inside. His hands were slick with sweat. He looked around the room—it was small, the décor authentic, as if they had stepped back into the nineteenth century—and then his eyes locked with hers.

They stood in silent communion, staring into each other's faces. Derek saw his own confusion mirrored in Ginny, the feeling that they should know each other, but that neither of them knew why. They might have remained there for hours if Ginny had not turned away.

"Melville kept John from coming into the house, so the young soldier ran down to the street and called out for Abby." Ginny pointed to the corner window. "She threw back the drapes, opened the glass, and they talked for hours—like Romeo and Juliet."

Derek's eyes strayed around the room, noticing the flowers. There were vases on the dressers, on the bedside tables, all filled with brightly colored bouquets.

Ginny smiled. "Beautiful, aren't they?"

He nodded.

"Melville kept turning John away, but the soldier bought Abby flowers and paid local children to deliver them for him, to let her know that he still loved her, that he hadn't abandoned her." Ginny stepped across the room to the window, her breath fogging the cold glass as she continued. "They say Melville finally murdered him, down there on the street, shot him in the stomach. John died looking up at the house, at this window, forever denied his one true love."

"What about Abby? What happened to her?"

"She saw the whole thing. With her soldier gone, there was no point in living. She... she hung herself." Ginny pointed to the far side of the room: a closet door. "In there."

Despite his coat, gooseflesh erupted on Derek's arms and neck.

"It wasn't long before the stories started," she told him. "People reported smelling flowers throughout the house, even in the middle of winter. Some claimed to have seen the girl standing here, gazing down at the street corner, still waiting for her soldier to return."

Her eyes lowered and her voice became distant.

"And then there are the noises."

"Noises?"

"From the closet, the sound of a hanging body swinging and slapping the walls: creak... thump... creak... thump.

"One of the owners grew so tired of hearing it, he actually boarded the closet up. It stayed that way for years, until the state bought the house and turned it into a museum."

Derek moved to the closet and opened it. A single bulb dangled on a cord, visible even in the gloom. He found a light switch and flicked it on. Round hatboxes sat on a shelf and empty hangers hung on the bar below. Apart from a few cobwebs, he saw nothing to inspire fear in anyone.

Ginny turned away from the window glass. "This house... you felt drawn to it, didn't you? Like you needed to be here?"

"Yes," he admitted, and it was as if a huge set of barbells lifted off his chest.

Ginny smiled. "Me, too, like I'd been here before. Like I... Like I belonged here."

"So... what?" He closed the closet door and moved away from it. "You think we're supposed to *be* them, Abby and John, reincarnated or possessed or..."

Ginny cut him off with her laughter. "Possessed?"

Derek smiled in spite of himself. "Sound's pretty crazy, doesn't it?"

She took a step toward him. "About as crazy as me asking a total stranger out on a date."

It's destiny, he thought dimly, surprised that the voice in his head was now his own.

"There's a restaurant just down the street," she told him, "Food & Friends. I have some work to do here, but if you'd like to get us a table, I can meet you there."

"I'd like that," he told her, his nervousness melting like frost before the dawn. "I'd like that a lot."

Derek followed Ginny down the stairs into the gift shop, then walked out into the cold. When he glanced back over his shoulder, he saw her standing at the window, smiling, a young woman looking at her soldier, her love.

He smiled back at her, then made his way down the path.

* * *

Ginny watched him walk away; each step remembered by the snow-covered trail. Cold seeped through the window glass into her bones. She shuddered, her smile withering like rose petals.

He will not set foot in this house again.

The declaration filled Ginny's inner ear; a stranger's voice, but she felt its anger and determination as if they were her own. She glanced over her shoulder, found the male portrait that hung above the fireplace. It stared back at her, into her, icy as the winter chill.

Ginny walked to the register, to the drawer hidden beneath. Her fingers slid inside, crawled through the darkness like a hungry spider, and when they found the .38-caliber pistol hidden within, they seized it.

He will not come near my niece.

She marched outside and hunted the soldier into the night.

Scott Nicholson
WAMPUS CAT

TRUE

SCOTT NICHOLSON is the author of seven novels, including *They Hunger* and *The Red Church*. He's also published more than 60 short stories and has written five screenplays and the *Dirt* graphic novel series. Nicholson's Web site is www.hauntedcomputer.com.

Susan should have known better than to head south with a man, especially to the place her grandmother called "the land of legends."

This was the dark heart of the Alleghenies and dusk was pumpkin colored, and the mountains stood like giant petrified beasts against the mist. Trees mingled, black sticks intersecting. The fallen leaves were as sodden as a fraternity carpet. October's rot filled the air.

And Barry was lost. Barry, with a forty-dollar compass and LL Bean hiking boots and a copy of Thoreau's *Walden* in his backpack, was so lost that Saturday morning looked like Tuesday night.

Susan should have said something. Maybe Saturday afternoon, when Barry eased his hook into the Shawneehaw. Barry had read a book on fly fishing, and Ted Williams, the greatest hitter in baseball history, was also a fly fisherman. Barry talked about Ted Williams so much that Susan wished Williams had been a Yankee instead of playing for the Red Sox.

Because Barry was Yankee. Maine Yankee, the worst kind. She

was Jersey Shore college by way of Piedmont Carolina, and much of her blood was rock-deep Southern Appalachian, Scots-Irish and paranoid, a little free-spirited and flaky, but that was no excuse to fall for him. He had passed himself off as a real man and reality was subject to change.

Not that all men should automatically be able to kill bears with a hatchet.

But they could at least take a little time and get things right. Like know where they were. And who they were with. To Barry, Susan might as well have been AnnaBeth-Mary, the previous temporary girlfriend to follow him on these Appalachian journeys.

Doubtless, others had preceded AnnaBeth-Mary and Susan. All of them falling in lock-step with Barry, because when the sun hit his hair just right, he glowed like a lion. Tall and tan and crisp, with muscles and a toothy smile.

But after a while, Barry's little flaws started to show. His confusion. His forgetfulness. His obsession with fly fishing. His play-by-play of the year Ted Williams hit .406.

By Sunday evening, Barry had completely thrown Susan over for the creek. Barry put on waist-high rubber trousers and headed for deep water. She watched from the boulders like a dismal cheerleader as currents swirled around his knees.

And Monday was just as dull. Susan read the hardback biography of Benjamin Franklin, a book thick enough to impress any man. But Barry stood by the fire with his fishing pole and a dumb grin, and he turned in early so he could chase fish for breakfast.

And now it was Tuesday evening, and they were lost.

"It's Monday, isn't it?" Barry said.

"It's Tuesday."

Barry nodded, fumbled through his backpack, and brought out his fancy bottled water. The campfire glinted off the plastic. Barry peered at the bottle. It was as vacant as his eyes.

"Are we in West Virginia or plain Virginia?" Susan hated herself for not knowing. They'd passed through Harper's Ferry and over the Shenandoah River, then up Loudon Heights where the trail maps showed a meandering thread back and forth across the border. They headed south out of survival instinct, toward warmer weather. Susan hadn't kept track of miles; all she knew was her feet were sore.

She could outwalk Barry any day, and she could pitch her tent faster than he did. Barry had no brain cells that weren't clouded by Ted Williams and trout and AnnaBeth-what's-her-name.

And now Susan was stuck with him.

In the mountains.

In the fog with dark coming on.

And it was Tuesday evening.

Late October.

In the southern Appalachian mountains.

Susan's grandma, who everybody called Mamaw, said the mountains were way wilder than what the movies said. The mountains weren't hillbilly dolls and moonshine stills. The mountains were old as time, and secrets slept under a mile of worn dirt. Mamaw said those who belonged to them always came back, because the trees and rocks and people and animals were all of the same blood, tapped into the same spirit. Mamaw told of the Wampus Cat, the creature that could change from a witch to a cat in order to seek its prey better, and how it had been caught in the middle of its transformation. Now, when the moon was full, it could be seen in human size, howling, dripping saliva from its fangs, its yellow eyes glowing in the fierce furry face.

Susan shook herself awake.

For the second time.

Cold.

Because Barry was curled and snoring in his little pup tent. And she had to use the bathroom—or in this case, the woods. Real bad.

The Appalachian twilight was scary, because she was from Gastonia. Dead factory town, lazy with the letter *a* and not too proud of it. The mountains were a myth that lay somewhere beyond the pollution belt, the land of legends. But in the dark, the legends seemed far too real. And Mamaw said legends didn't lie. And dogs didn't like Mamaw.

Susan shook Barry's tent. "I've got to go."

"Snurk?"

She shook again. "I've got to go out in the woods. And it's getting dark."

Barry stuck his head out of the tent.

"Sorry, AnnaBeth," he said.

"I'm Susan."

"Sorry."

Men were always sorry.

Especially Barry.

"I've got to go behind a tree. And I don't want to go out there alone." Susan could walk the back streets in factory towns, roll miles on a city subway, take a plane to Pensacola. But the West Virginia woods were a different story. Or were these the Virginia woods?

Barry groaned and crawled out of the tent. He stumbled, groggy from sleep, and went to the fire. He busied himself throwing wood on the pile of embers while she sneaked behind the nearest oak.

As she relieved herself, the chirping of the crickets rose in an uneven symphony. Mamaw said the animals knew songs older than the creek music that trickled between high boulders. And they sang louder in late October, when the magic inside the world seeped closer to the outer skin. Susan heard something in the brush and wiped and zipped before she was completely finished.

Barry sat on a big rock by the fire. The firelight cast him in bronze, and he looked attractive again. Then he belched and the wind changed and smoke drifted into Susan's face. She sat on the ground across from him, as far away as she could manage without freezing to death.

"Are we near Shepherdstown?" she asked. Because Shepherdstown was a real place, a dot on the map, and no doubt had some kind of fast-food franchise. If she ate another handful of honey-sweetened rolled oats, she was going to turn into a diabetic horse.

Barry pulled his compass from his belt. His golden brow furrowed. On Saturday, such a simple gesture would have set her shivering with love. Now she wanted to pull his ears down over his head and cram his compass into his nose.

Barry tapped the compass and rubbed the stubble on his chin. "I think so."

Barry said *think* with the old Barryesque self-confidence. Even in doubt, he was never wrong.

Susan counted the days backwards on her fingers. "We left on the twenty-seventh, right?"

"Yeah. Parked the car in Maryland. Greenbrier, wasn't it?" He patted his pocket to make sure he still had the keys. She should have paid attention to little dissonant clues like the Green Party sticker on the bumper of his gas-hog SUV. Clues like AnnaBeth-Mary's picture taped to the dashboard. But, on October twenty-seventh, Susan couldn't see beyond his blue eyes.

"That makes tonight Halloween," she said.

"Halloween?" His expression switched from confusion to glee.

She looked around at the trees. Had the crickets fallen silent? She shifted closer to the fire. "And we're lost."

"We're not lost."

"Where are we, then?"

Barry waved his hands at the woods surrounding them. "Here. Near Shepherdstown."

Nowhere. With night sliding from the trees like sick shadows.

Barry must have mistaken her look of concern for come-hither. He lowered his voice, the way he'd probably heard George Clooney do it in a movie. "And it's just the two of us, honey. Trick or treat."

Yes, just Barry and Susan. Or was it AnnaBeth-Mary, or maybe the half-dozen other girls Barry had mentioned on the drive down south? Mamaw said you were never alone in the mountains, because the woods watched you like a hungry beast. And legends never lied—

Two golden specks flashed against the black face of the forest. Susan shifted closer to the fire. "Did you see that?"

"Huh?"

"ABright. Like animal eyes."

"Might be a deer. Or a raccoon. Coons like to prowl around campsites."

"These eyes were yellow."

"Probably just a reflection of the fire."

Except the fire was mostly orange and red. Not deep yellow like the eyes. And Mamaw said the mountains had eyes, they watched and they waited, and them that belonged always came back.

Barry grinned with those perfect teeth and moved to Susan's side, dragging the backpack. He rummaged in a zippered pouch and brought out a cigarette. He lit it and passed it to her, but she shook her head.

"I'm scared of cancer."

He took another drag and put his arm around her. "Don't be scared. I'll protect you."

She was wondering who was going to protect her from Barry. That's when the branch snapped. She hated herself for it, but she snuggled closer to Barry. Mamaw and her stories. Always told as if the strange were true. "That sounded way too big for a raccoon."

"Noise carries funny in the mountains, especially at night."

"Do they have bears up here?" Mamaw said bears were almost as bad as the big mountain cats, the *painters*, what had big fangs and screamed like women in the hurt of childbirth. But nothing compared to a vengeful and angry Wampus Cat.

Barry gave his hiccup of a laugh. "The Smoky Mountains have more black bears than you can shake a stick at. Huh-huh. Smoky." He stubbed out the cigarette.

"According to the guidebook, this is the Shenandoah National Forest, not the Smokies."

"Whatever. Mountains are mountains."

Her tent looked inviting, but if she crawled inside, she'd be trapped. And the canvas walls looked far too flimsy to hold back a large animal. Or the weight of the mountains. Or the strength of legends.

"Say, I know a good ghost story," Barry said.

"I don't want to hear any ghost stories."

"Hey, come on. It's Halloween."

How could she tell him what a jerk he was without insulting him and losing what little comfort he offered? As much as she hated to admit it, she needed him. At least until they reached civilization, at which point she would happily give back his twangy bluegrass CDs and never speak to him again. He could drive north, she could head south, and the mountains would forget them, go on with the business of being ancient and full of secrets.

The noise came again, louder and to Susan's left. "Did you hear it that time?"

Barry pointed up through the gap in the trees. "Moon's almost full."

"On Halloween."

"You don't believe in that kind of junk, do you?"

"Spooks and goblins?" she said. "No, not when I'm safe in bed with a deadbolt on the door and the radio going. But out here, it's different. And you never heard Mamaw's stories."

Stories about the lady with the lamp, who glowed by the river; painters who followed the wood wagon home, screaming all the way; fireflies that stabbed a billion sparks above the creek beds; frost that glittered in the soft ghost breath of morning; legends that grew legs and flesh and teeth and walked the Southern hills. Stuff that got in your blood and owned you.

"These mountains are alive." Barry's idea of poetry. Or his way of scaring her. All the same, with Barry.

"I don't want to hear any more strange noises, thank you." Susan would not allow this idiot to hear her whine. Her discomfort was genuine, deeper than ancient granite and Mamaw's long line of handed-down stories. "And I don't want to see yellow eyes in the forest. All I want is a hot bath and a greasy hamburger and some clean sheets."

Barry tried to look wounded, but the expression came off as something an inept president might hide behind during a press conference. He took his arm from her shoulders.

"I thought you were an Earth chick," he said.

"I'm not a chick in any sense of the word. I'm not going to grow up to be a hen, and roosters hold absolutely no appeal. But I'm about ready to ruffle some feathers."

"Don't be like that."

She started to pour it on, dump eighty miles of hiking and their being lost and his two-track-mindedness on him and probably she would end up crying in frustration except, before she could really get rolling, she saw the yellow eyes again.

In front of them, maybe fifteen feet away.

This time, even Barry saw them.

"What was that?" He stood and grabbed a long limb from the fire, held it as a torch.

The eyes disappeared in blackness.

"That wasn't a reflection." Susan picked up the closest rock.

"Looked like yellow eyes to me."

"I told you."

"Shh." Barry waved his hand.

The noise came from the left. And the right. And behind them.

Susan turned her back to the fire. The rock was heavy in her hand. The only direction that didn't seem scary was up, with the stars blind in the glow of the moon. Mamaw said the sky hung heavier in the mountains, that it took your breath and then your soul, because you're closer to heaven here.

The eyes flashed beside her tent. Branches broke. The laughter of wind swept from the trees.

Halloween. Trick or treat. In the land of legends. Mamaw's territory.

The campfire grabbed some oxygen and jumped for the sky. Smoke burned Susan's eyes and nose. The forest grew wild, unafraid, with Appalachian teeth.

The night swooped in like bats, the trees bent with knotted limbs, the golden eyes closed in. It was coming, whatever it was.

Susan raised the rock. "Barry!"

He jumped in front of her and waved the burning stick as if it were a flag. Embers fell from its tip. He shouted at the woods. The eyes froze, then faded back to invisibility.

The air grew still again. The fire sputtered. Leaves settled on the ground. Susan's heart, the one Barry had briefly stolen, was now back and working overtime.

She should have known better than to head south with a man. Not into this land that Mamaw said was haunted by ancient things. Especially not on Halloween.

"What was it?" Susan's hands were cold.

Barry had long lost his glow, was now just another guy with body odor and the deep-seated fear that all guys tried to hide but was always just a sniff away. He tugged at the waistband of his jeans. "Mountain lion, I bet."

"Mountain lion? The guidebook didn't say anything about mountain lions."

Barry tried to ruralize his speech, hard to do with the nasally Maine accent. "Supposed to be extinct in these parts. But there's a lot about these woods that people don't know."

"I know, I know, the land of legends." Susan edged closer to the fire. It was burning low. Somebody would have to go in search of wood. Somebody named Barry.

"Big cats, they'll come right up to a camp. They're not afraid."

"Barry, stop trying to scare me."

He grinned. "Best thing to do is get in the tent and hope it goes away."

"The fire's dying."

"So?" He crawled into his tent.

Susan looked around at the woods. Painters could climb trees, couldn't they? Were they afraid of fire? What color eyes did they have? All the cats Susan knew had golden or green or gray eyes, but those were house cats. Maybe mountain lions were different.

Bigger.

Wild things in the land of legends.

Creatures with fang and claw that had stalked here long before the Catawba and Cherokee and Algonquin, long before the Scottish and Irish and German settlers, and long before Daniel Boone, that original tourist, had started the southern Appalachians on its downward cultural slide. The guidebook writers from New York couldn't know much about mountain lions, painters, and distant legends. And absolutely nothing about Wampus Cats that were forever locked in transformation, caught between two worlds.

Something chuckled in the dark, and it sure wasn't the ghost of Daniel Boone.

Even though this was Halloween.

When midnight made promises.

Susan didn't wait for the yellow eyes to appear. The wet rustling of leaves was all the encouragement she needed. Still clutching the rock, she scrambled into her tent. She listened closely to the quiet. To Tuesday night. To October.

To Halloween.

To a mountain lion that shouldn't exist.

The creature's silhouette was now clear, black against the amber glow of the fading fire.

"Williams faced the Yankees thirteen times in 1941," Barry said from the neighboring tent.

"Barry." She wasn't sure if she had mustered enough air to summon this lost fool of the wilderness. She tried again, glad she had a rock in her hand.

He grunted, already half asleep.

"Barry!" The shadow was bigger now. Something nuzzled her tent flaps.

Something with long whiskers.

And October teeth.

The fire died.

Susan was alone with the night. And a snoring Barry. And whatever was outside. In Mamaw's land.

She held her breath, hoping it would go away.

It didn't.

She listened to the breathing of the big mountain cat. Soft, at home in the darkness. At ease. Something that belonged in the land of legends.

Barry would protect her. Barry would growl and grab a stick and scream stupid words at the stars.

And the cat would . . . what?

Barry's uneven snoring was an insult to the crickets.

Susan lay on her belly, ear at the entrance to the tent.

The woods sang a mountain song, of Rebel yells and squirrels and rustling laurel thickets. Creeks ran quick and cold in the dark. A cat purred, patient as the moon. Mamaw's ghost sang a lost ballad of wind in the woods.

Susan whispered Barry's name, afraid the cat would hear. She flicked on her flashlight, pulled down the zipper of the tent, and peered through the nylon netting. More fervid eyes waited in the October blackness. More mountain lions that shouldn't exist. More wild things. More of Mamaw's painters. And behind them, a Wampus Cat mewling a folk hymn.

She had been wrong all along. Because Barry had seemed like the wild thing, a beast that she must tame or die trying.

Now she saw that he was the danger. He was tame, and his tameness would build a cage around her. His world was one of baseball statistics and environmental rallies and kayaks and snowboards and an endless stream of trail girls, not rocks and trees. He entered this land of legends like a conqueror, with bottled water and wool socks and Yankee pride.

Deliverance wasn't a documentary. The southern Appalachians weren't savage and cruel. The mountains only resisted what didn't belong here. And maybe she belonged, her blood thick through three generations, Mamaw's heart still beating in hers. A witch's spell stretching over generations.

The night chill fell away as she left the camp. The eyes surrounded her, warm breath touched her skin, soft paws played at the ground. This was Halloween, a night of trick or treat, when legends came alive. And the legends had come for her.

The forest called, the mountains waited, the wilderness sent an invitation. Mamaw's song drifted between the trees, beckoning, haunting, welcoming, with a chorus of "Follow your heart."

Her heart was full of the scent of Barry, the stench of his too-human flesh, and her teeth ached for his taste. But he would be easy to track later. For now, the night beckoned.

Susan ran with the painters, free.

Somewhere in the night she changed. At least, half of her did.

John R. Little
GEORGE'S HEAD

JOHN R. LITTLE won a 2008 Bram Stoker award for his novella *Miranda*. His earlier novel, *The Memory Tree*, was a Stoker finalist. His most recent book is *The Gray Zone*, recently published by Bad Moon Books. Upcoming is a short novel, *Dreams in Black and White*, from Morning Star Books. John is currently working on a new novel. You can visit his web site at www.johnrlittle.com to see writing updates. Feel free to email him with your thoughts on this story at john@johnrlittle.com.

Emma Nicole Smuck sat on a boulder near the river and lay her fishing rod on the ground. Her little sister, Sammy, had gotten bored and left to walk back to the farm house and the sun was starting to go down. Emma had been out at the bank for three hours with barely a nibble.

"Stupid fish," she said.

It was Emma's 12th birthday and when her mom asked what she'd wanted, all she could think of was a new fishing pole. It was waiting for her that morning, a shiny bright red rod with a slick reel and a brand new spool of twenty pound test line.

The perfect rod.

Too bad the fish didn't know that.

The water rushed by and Emma stared into the water. The river wasn't deep, nor was it very wide, only about twenty-five feet across, but in her imagination it was the mighty Mississippi, full of jumping catfish and trout.

Something glinted. She saw it from the corner of her eye, but when she looked directly at the spot, she saw nothing.

She moved her head a bit, left and right, and . . .

There!

It was on the far bank. Shiny. Not shiny like a mirror but more like snow reflecting the sunlight on a cold winter's day.

"Emma? What's wrong?"

"Sammy? I thought you went back home."

She shrugged. Sammy had her own fishing rod. Well, it was Emma's old rod, a flimsy pole made of bamboo. Gramps had made it for Emma, so she liked it and everything, but she was glad it was time to hand it down to Sammy. In four years, when Sammy was twelve, maybe she'd want a nice rod, too. Or maybe not. She hadn't seemed very interested today.

"Scardy cat."

"Am not."

Emma shrugged and moved her dark hair back over her shoulders. She and Sammy were like identical twins born four years apart. Same coal black hair, same green eyes, same smile and laugh.

Emma looked back and saw the spark of reflected sunlight again.

"What are you looking at?" asked Sammy.

"I don't know. But I'm going to get it."

"Where?"

"Across the other side."

"I don't see anything."

Emma pointed at the small white patch buried in the bank. She wouldn't have seen it most years, but the drought this spring had lowered the river level.

She took her shoes and socks off and rolled up her pant legs to her knees. As she walked across, she found the river was deeper than she thought and much more powerful. Her pants were getting soaked. She kept walking and the water was up to her waist. It took all her concentration to not lose her footing.

"Mom won't like that!"

Emma waved back at Sammy and continued. No point going back now. Not with her sister watching her, anyhow.

The water was cold, and Emma tried to move a bit faster, but it felt like she was walking through molasses as she fought the current.

"Finally," she said as she reached the other side.

The white thing was hard, like rock, and it was buried deep in the bank. She used her fingers to scrape all the dirt away and freed it. It finally popped out of the muck, and Emma screamed.

Sammy yelled, "What happened?"

Emma dropped the skull into the river and lost her footing but recovered soon enough. She looked around in fear but saw nothing threatening. Her T-shirt was now soaked along with her pants.

"Emma, what was it?"

She reached into the water to find the skull and held it over her head.

Sammy stared silently at the clean white skull in Emma's hand.

Emma turned it and held it to her face to get a better look. The jawbone was missing, but she could see a top row of teeth still there. It looked like the skull was staring at her. A chill seemed to run down her spine and for a second she thought of tossing the thing away.

"Spooky."

The surface of the skull was grainy, not smooth, and she wondered if it could possibly be real. *Probably not*, she decided.

Still, it'd make a cool addition to her desk. She could tell stories of it being a long-dead relative, and who could say otherwise?

"Em . . . Help."

Emma kept staring at the skull when she heard the tiny call from her sister.

"Sammy? What's wrong? It can't hurt you. It's probably just a fake."

"No! It's real!"

Emma looked at Sammy, wondering why her voice had such a tone of urgency.

There was nothing unusual going on. Sammy just stood on the opposite bank of the river, maybe hunched over a bit but otherwise just fine.

Sammy looked up for a few seconds and then yelled over to Emma. "You have to bring the skull over here right now!"

"What are you talking about?"

"There's a guy here. He needs his head back. He's like a ghost or something. He's grabbing my shoulder and he's scaring me, Em."

Emma shook her head and watched the water roaring past her. She'd had no trouble getting across but she was so focused on the skull, she hadn't realized how deep the water was. Now that she knew, well, it looked harder to get back. Especially carrying the stupid fake skull.

"There's no such thing as ghosts," she called.

Emma stared at the skull again. Was it real? She didn't know what a real skull would look like. It's probably just a stupid toy.

"Em! His name is George Van Meter. He says Indians cut his head off and he's been looking for it ever since. He says that's *his* skull, and he needs you to bring it back to him!"

Sammy's shriek made Emma look back at her little sister.

"What's *wrong?*"

Sammy was breathing too fast, hyperventilating.

"Sammy!! Tell me!"

"He's going to take me away if you don't give him the skull back! Em, he's pressing his hands on my neck. Hard! Help!"

"Sammy, cut it out. You're bugging me. I'm coming back."

She took a few steps forward, each one making her feel more weak than the one before. The river rushed at her and for a split second, she imagined herself being swept off her feet and carried downstate. Somebody would find her corpse miles away.

She felt her foot slip on a stone and then she did fall. The water was about three feet deep here, and she found herself grasping at rocks with both hands to stop herself from being swept away. The river was as ferocious as the Niagara, as wide as the Amazon. She panicked and found herself spitting out water and shaking her head as she sat on her knees.

"Emma..."

Sammy's voice was softer, but Emma didn't have time to worry about that. She needed to get across the river.

The skull was gone. She'd let go when she fell and it was nowhere to be seen.

"I'm coming, Sammy. Hold on."

This time there was no reply. Emma blinked water from her eyes and looked across the water. Sammy wasn't there.

She rushed through the rest of the water, not caring about slipping anymore, and as a result, she was sure-footed and reached the other side in a few seconds.

"Sammy!"

She went to where her sister had been standing, and saw only blood-stained sand. The blood was still wet.

There was too much of it. There was no other sign of Sammy.

A vision of the skull flashed through her mind, but it vanished as she ran to her house, screaming for her mom.

Brian J. Hatcher
A BANSHEE IN BECKLEY

BRIAN J. HATCHER is an author and poet from Charleston, WV. He has appeared in the two previous volumes of *Legends of the Mountain State*, as well as *Weird Tales Magazine* and the upcoming poetry anthology *Leonard Cohen: You're Our Man*. Information about the author, along with his video blog, Brian With An "Eye", can be found on his website at BrianJHatcher.com.

My hospital bed is a restless nest of wires and tubes, yet I feel myself connected to nothing but the past. It's the height of summer, but all I can think about is Christmas. Not this coming Christmas, although I would give just about anything to see it. I don't look forward to Christmas; I always look back—to 1987. Not because it was the last real Christmas I'd ever know, not because Squeaky Fromme escaped from Alderson Prison that year, and not because of a guilt that has lurked in the periphery of my thoughts for most of my life. I remember that Christmas because of the tears, the same tears that may soon be shed for me.

The winter of 1987 was my sophomore year in college. Two days before Christmas, I went home to be with my family. The trip by Greyhound, including stops, was fourteen hours and all night long. The bus rumbled along the midnight highway but no one slept, because of that woman. I saw her only in profile from the other side of the aisle and a few seats in front of me, talking to a friend I couldn't see in a voice not quite soft enough to be considerate. When the woman pulled out a newspaper and started flipping through it, I hoped it would keep her quiet long enough to take a nap. No such luck. The woman screeched and the paper rustled as she pushed it over to her friend. "Look at this! My girl Squeaky got out!"

The same day I bought my bus ticket to come home, Lynne "Squeaky" Fromme had escaped from the Alderson Federal Prison Camp. The authorities recaptured her on Christmas Day, but by then I would be more concerned with other matters.

I knew all about Squeaky Fromme. As a youngster, I had an interest in true crime. I collected stories about Jack the Ripper, Albert Fish, and the Boston Strangler, but I was especially interested in Charles Manson. His and Squeaky's connection to West Virginia made them, in my eyes, sort of perverse local legends.

Growing up, I spent many summers at my grandpa's house in Beckley. Grandpa Colin had been an unrepentant gear head for as long as I'd known him. I'd help him fix cars, but I never really enjoyed the work. I hated the feel of the thick grease between my fingers. But I liked hanging out with Grandpa.

One summer I was helping Grandpa pull the carburetor from a '71 Plymouth Barracuda. It was 1974, the year Bugliosi's book on Manson came out. I was telling Grandpa every detail I'd gleaned from reading it. He listened patiently while I rambled on about Charles Manson.

"Think about it," I said. "If Manson hadn't gone to California and met the Family, he wouldn't even be in prison."

Grandpa loosened the carburetor valve with the tip of a flathead screwdriver. "Oh, I think he'd have gone back to jail, lad. If not for that, then something else." I can still hear his voice. He came to America from Scotland when he was eight. His brogue softened with time, but never completely went away.

"Why do you say that?" I asked.

Grandpa put down the screwdriver. "Well, I suppose you're old enough to know. I met Charlie Manson in Federal Reformatory at Chillicothe. They transferred him a few months before I was paroled."

"You never told me you went to jail. What for?"

"When I was young, a bunch of us teenagers would go across the state line and steal cars. We'd bring them back into West Virginia, strip them, and sell them for parts. First it was for kicks. But then I married your grandma, and she was pregnant with your mother, so I did it to feed my family, although I never told your grandma where I got the extra cash.

"One day my luck ran out. Two State Troopers caught me breaking into a car outside Columbus. I tried to take off but they caught me. I got ten years. And that's how I met Charlie Manson. He went to jail for stealing cars, just like me."

"What was he like?"

"A model prisoner. He wanted to put in good time and get out. I figure he knew if he didn't straighten up he'd spend the rest of his life behind bars."

"Guess he didn't do so well," I said.

"I didn't think he would. From the moment I saw him, he had the weight of inevitability about him. I somehow knew that man would spend the rest of his life in prison. As for me, I didn't want to end up the same way, so I made sure when I got out that I stayed out. Your grandma waited for me. Why, I don't know. It still took her a long time to trust me again. But finally, she did. Maybe she saw something in me, like I saw something else in Manson. But I still paid a price. I wasn't there for my daughter's birth. She was almost a teenager when I got out and I missed seeing her grow up. That's the lesson, lad. Don't waste life. You don't ever know how much of it you'll have."

"And all this time Grandma never said anything about it."

"She wanted to put it all behind us. She was afraid people would think differently of us if they knew my past. To tell the truth, I'm not so sure she'd like that I told you. Let's just keep this between you and me, what do you say?"

"I won't say a word."

I meant to keep my promise, but I was still young. I told my friends at school about Grandpa and Charlie Manson. I thought they'd think it was cool, like I did. I regretted it later. Although no one believed me, I felt I had betrayed Grandpa's trust. That guilt followed me most of my young life.

After that summer afternoon, Grandpa would tell me stories about ghosts and monsters that supposedly inhabited West Virginia. The Mothman, Screaming Jenny, and dozens of other stories. I guess he figured those monsters were better for me than the real ones I found so interesting. His favorite story was about the Marrtown Banshee. It was a part of Scotland transplanted into West Virginia, just like him. I would humor him and listen to his stories, but by then my attention had turned from serial killers to girls. Go figure.

The Greyhound bus rolled into the Beckley station at 3:34 in the morning, almost a half an hour early but still four hours before anyone would be there to pick me up. I told everyone my bus would arrive around 7:30. I didn't want anyone dragging themselves out of bed just to get me. Still, sitting in those hard plastic chairs to wait didn't appeal to me, so I went outside to smoke. I had two Marlboros left in the pack and I planned to smoke them both. No one in my family knew I smoked, and I wanted to keep it that way.

I went around the side of the building and lit up. I hotboxed the first one down to the filter; it had been a long bus ride. I smoked the second about halfway when I heard something across the street. There was a woman huddled under the awning of the closed convenient store, crying.

I crossed the street to check on her. She had the reddest hair I'd ever seen curling over her face. She was sobbing uncontrollably.

"Miss, are you okay? Do you need me to call someone?"

I wasn't sure she heard me. She kept crying into her hands. "Oh, me poor Colin! Me poor sweet Colin!" Her thick Scottish accent warbled from her sobs.

"What's wrong?" I asked.

"He's dyin'. Soon he'll be cold and dead. Me poor sweet Colin!"

I remembered a story Grandpa told me, almost immediately. "My . . . Grandpa's name is Colin."

The woman looked right at me. Her eyes were large and green, and bloodshot from tears. "Aye," she said. "I cry for him. And one day, lad, I'll cry for ye, too."

She turned to leave. I reached out to her, and my hand touched nothing. She disappeared right in front of me, and I felt lightheaded as if suddenly waking from a dream. Yet in the distance, I could still hear her sobbing.

I tossed the rest of my cigarette away and went back to the bus station to get warm. Grandpa was just inside the door. "There you are, lad. Where did you get off to?"

"What are you doing here?"

Grandpa smiled. "I know how to read a bus schedule, if you had any doubts. So where were you?"

"Me? Oh, I just went outside for some fresh air."

"Ah, so that's why your clothes smell of cigarettes. People go around the building to smoke, and you probably leaned up against a wall and got it all over you. Let's get you back to the house so you can change. We wouldn't want anyone to get the wrong idea. Okay, lad?"

There was no fooling Grandpa, ever. "Okay."

Grandpa's house was twenty minutes away from the bus station. I looked up the hill as we drove passed Park Junior High. Grandpa interrupted the swirling thoughts of my childhood. "Guess what? Your grandpa's going to be a writer."

"Really? What are you writing?"

"You remember all the stories I used to tell when you were young. I'm putting a book together of West Virginia legends and ghost stories. I even have a local publisher interested."

"That's great, Grandpa."

"It's a lot of hard work, though. I wanted to write the stories as they were told, not just how I remembered them. I've talked to a lot of people. I was on the phone for an hour last week with one of the Marrs family. You remember that story, don't you?"

Of course, I did. "Grandpa, do you think our family has a banshee?"

"It's possible," Grandpa said. "I had a great-great aunt who died in childbirth. Had the reddest hair anyone had ever seen, so I'm told. If anyone came back as our family's banshee, it would be her."

I didn't say anything.

"Something bothering you, lad?"

At the time I didn't know why, but I told Grandpa about the crying woman.

He didn't say anything at first. Then he sighed and said, "Ah, well, lad. Isn't life always just like that?"

Neither Grandpa nor I said anything more about it, to anyone. On Christmas Day, Grandpa went up to take a nap. He never woke up.

There were no more Christmases at Grandpa's. Or anywhere else for me.

For a long time I wondered that, if I hadn't said anything, if maybe Grandpa might have lived. I felt like I had betrayed him all over again. I carried that guilt most of my life. But now, I don't think keeping quiet would have changed anything. I believe the reason I told him that night was because I saw the weight of inevitability about him. The same weight I feel now.

When I came home from Grandpa's funeral, still mourning his death and the book he would never write, I sat in the swing in the back yard. Grandpa used to push me in that swing. I rocked gently for a while, but stopped when I heard something in the woods. Over the hissing of the wind in the trees, I could hear the banshee weeping again, although I couldn't see her. I haven't thought about that in years. I can't help but think of it now.

Since I've been in the hospital, I haven't had visitors. My parents died years ago, and I'm the last of my clan. The nurses are polite but guarded. They haven't told me anything yet, but I get the message and it isn't hopeful. My Grandpa died of his first heart attack. My first one put me in the hospital two days ago. My second one was last night.

I'm forty-two. I'm still young enough to get married, have children, do all those things I thought I had time for. I have plans. Grandpa had plans. Everyone has plans.

Sometimes I can't stop crying. Maybe somewhere the banshee cries for me, too, like she promised. I'm afraid to die. But what scares me more is that I don't know if there's anyone left to hear the banshee crying, for either of our sakes. And when I'm gone, who will she cry for then?

A Banshee in Beckley

Kelli Dunlap
CALLING THE DEAD

KELLI DUNLAP resides in Pennsylvania with her two children, a needy cat and some hippie. She spends her days paying the bills and free time writing, reading and/or editing for several popular midlist genre authors. Several shorts are available this year, she will be appearing in three anthologies next year, and of course, her first novel will be available this winter from Morning Star, an imprint of Bloodletting Press. Visit her at www.kellidunlap.com to stalk her, er, I mean for more information.

Justin threw the basketball at the hoop without aiming, and it ricocheted back at him from the backboard. Lately, he had been more consumed with self-pity and rage than anything else, and most of that was aimed at his mother. He hated her for moving him across country. Hated how she assumed she knew what was best for him. Hated leaving lifelong classmates and friends his senior year, arguing against her rationalization of cell phones and email options. Most of all he hated understanding why she had done it.

Justin threw the ball again, noting the park's small playground and family area—complete with grills and picnic tables—were all but empty. His mother had told him to make friends. He just wanted to be left alone. He would have been, and it would have been perfect, except for the two kids sitting atop one of the tables. He realized they were telling each other overexaggerated ghost stories and felt his anger surface again, directed, as the shrinks would say, inappropriately. So he blurted the first thing that came to mind that he thought might shut them up.

"I found a dead body last year."

At fourteen he may have fed into the self-imposed fear and enjoyed the tales. Heck, at seventeen he may have. But after the reality of last fall, fiction and fable were trumped by the discovery of a girl he knew. When he found her, Julie wasn't what he remembered, what he'd known. She wasn't the girl he'd called every day and skipped practice to hang out with. She wasn't the girl he'd been hoping would see him as more than a friend. She was gone. Brutally murdered. And what remained was only discernable by the homemade cross tattooed on her ankle. Ghost stories were childish in the aftermath of police reports, therapists, and medication.

"Yeah, right." The kid with the backward ball cap sneered at him, cocking his head to the side.

"Oh no, I did." Justin turned to face them fully. "That's why my mom moved us to this godforsaken place." He couldn't help but stare at the girl that reminded him a little too much of one he once knew, one he missed. Her blonde hair was pulled into a tight ponytail and she hid her figure under a football jersey, but it did nothing to hide the long tan legs—devoid of any hand-done ink jobs.

"Gross." She leaned forward and the curiosity in her eyes betrayed her words. "What'd they look like when you found them? Was it bloated? Did it smell bad? Oh hey, I'm Gina. Ignore Cody, he's just being an idiot. "

Justin wasn't sure if she had taken a breath in the onslaught of questions and comments, but the lilt in her rapid-fire chatter made him smile, even as the questions flipped his stomach. He lifted a foot to rest on the bench seat and tried to steer the conversation elsewhere, suddenly uncomfortable on this topic. "Aren't you guys a little old for ghost stories? What grade are you in?"

Gina answered, "Eleventh this coming fall. And when you live *here*, you're never too old."

"Oh yeah?" He glanced at each looking for a smirk or other sign that it was a joke on the new kid. "What's so special about here?"

"Dude, you're in the Mountain State."

Justin was surprised Cody hadn't added "duh" to the end of the comment.

"And?" He played dumb, but knew better. He watched the specials on hauntings and poltergeists, he knew West Virginia was rich with history.

"Tons of stories around this state." Gina leaned back again and looked him up and down.

"Yeah, but you guys were talking about *your cousin's neighbor's ex-girlfriend heard this*, or something from *way down south, deep in the mountains*. What about here? If this state is so haunted, what happens here?"

Dark concern swirled in Gina's deep brown eyes.

"You never speak of what's close by. Ever." Cody's hushed words were raspy, desperate. "You wake things up that way. Things better left alone."

"You guys watch too much TV. . . or not enough. Ghost hunters go searching all the time. Equipment and cameras. They never find anything. Never *wake anything up*."

"Cody's right. . ." Gina raised an eyebrow at him. "You don't mess with what's in your own backyard."

"Fine. Just give me the basics. What do you have here?"

"Nothing any more." Cody's gaze locked on something over Justin's shoulder. Justin turned to see what the boy was looking at but saw nothing except a railroad track and field of grass.

"Haunted tracks?"

"Nah, the ballfield." If Justin believed teens were capable of reverence outside heroes, comics and boobs, he would have thought it was genuine sadness in Cody's voice. Instead he chalked it up to a lifetime of hearing local legends and the immaturity to shake the fear they created.

"Ballfield, eh?"

"Yeah. But we don't talk about it." Gina looked up from the ground. "The man that haunted the stands hasn't been around seen since they tore it down."

"So he's sleeping? Ghosts sleep? And you might wake him by talking about it?" Justin curled a lip in disbelief. "Yeah, right."

"You ever do Bloody Mary?" Cody's voice remained low and serious, giving him an embodiment beyond his age.

"No." Justin would never dream of it on principle, but decided he should downplay it. "It's stupid and doesn't work."

"How do you know? You ever tried?"

"What's that got to do with your guy?"

"Nothing. Everything." Cody slipped off the picnic table and stood to look Justin in the eye. "You think you're brave enough to do Bloody Mary on a dare?"

"On a dare, sure. But just for giggles? What's the point?"

"Well then, why not go see if you can wake up Jacob the same way? Cuz we're sure not going to do it." He nodded to Gina, and she stood to follow him.

"How am I supposed to do that? I don't know anything about him."

"Yeah? How much you know about Bloody Mary?"

Good point, thought Justin. "How about a little info? How old was he? What should I expect? Was he dangerous?"

"Nah. . . A harmless old man. Just sat and watched the games. But they said that if you acknowledged him, looked at him or tried to speak to him, then you'd wake—"

"Gina!" Cody grabbed her arm and Gina pulled back, shooting

Cody a look of anger. Her expression softened, she nodded slightly and then turned back to Justin.

"Good luck." Gina's words were positive, but her tone was a knowing good-bye, as if she were never going to see him again.

They walked away and Justin's mind reeled about the possibilities. He hadn't grown up with a local ghost story, but these kids had seemed very serious about waking the local dead, and that only heightened Justin's curiosity.

He looked in the direction they had indicated. The tracks were clear but beyond looked like an ordinary field. He squinted against the sun and saw the bald patches where the bases had been and the grass had given up hope over the years. They hadn't mentioned when it was torn down, but it couldn't have been too long ago for the grass to still be missing in those places. His feet moved before he had fully made up his mind to check out the legend, and he found himself at the railroad tracks before he knew it.

He thought of the television shows he'd watched and books he'd read and wondered if he could make it work just like Bloody Mary.

Call the dead and they will answer?

Okay, he thought. *What is going on?* And crossed the tracks to the field, wondering how many people had watched the games from this spot instead of in the stands. He opened up his senses on the way, like he'd seen them do on television, yet felt nothing when his feet hit the outfield. There was no gust of cold air or shiver down his spine when his worn sneakers crossed the grass that marked the baseline. There was just nothing here, to fear or otherwise, and he boldly walked to home plate.

Justin stood in the bare dirt where the stands used to be. He closed his eyes and imagined the field in its glory. The smell of hot dogs and feel of summer heat. The sound of the crowd, cheering and chattering. He envisioned the people in the stands, a full house, and began to pick out the real ones. The parents, brothers and girlfriends were checked off as he went through the crowd in his head. He looked at their faces, their clothes, their colors. He expected the old man to be faded or dated somehow. He figured he could pick him out of the crowd as he whittled through the fans. Justin fully expected this to work. He truly believed he could call the phantom to mind and make him bend to his will. He'd read enough, he'd watched enough.

And he should have therefore known the truth.

People don't find ghosts. Ghosts find them.

He scoured the stands for the old man, but a voice interrupted his imagined scene. A voice he knew. A voice he'd tried to forget.

"Justin." His eyes flew open and the stands were gone. The sound of an extra inning was replaced with his own scream.

He scrambled backward to escape the vision in front of him—the vision he'd been trying to exorcise from his nightmares—and fell to the ground, his tailbone landing on a sharp rock.

"Nooo. . ." He looked up to the vision in front of him, and months of doctors, drugs and hope were wiped out of existence.

"Justin..." She repeated through cracked lips that had continued to blacken since he'd seen them, as if she were still decomposing in his imagination. *Because that's what this had to be, it couldn't be real.*

And then she reached forward and touched him.

The shiver up his spine that had eluded him while hunting a ghost he didn't know, hit him full force when the one he'd moved to avoid reached out a bruised hand. He pulled back from her touch. Justin's mind reeled. He couldn't fathom how she'd crossed several states and why she'd come from the grave to find him. He hadn't hurt her. He had only found her.

And when he had, she had been intact except one finger, and been a deathly shade of blood-smeared gray. Now, her skin was covered in splotchy bruising, with white areas that reminded him of freezer burn on chocolate. Her nails had dried and splintered, breaking deep into the beds with several missing all together. Her left eye was the color of cake batter. Her right eye was missing, and in its place was what seemed to be a never-ending trickle of bile-colored mucus. Her green tear was incapable of conveying sympathy, as the sheer reality of it scared Justin into a speechless, teeth-chattering child that begged his own mind for logic to explain the phantom in front of him. She dragged a broken leg as she stepped forward, her denim shorts muddied—their stone-washing replaced with a thin sheen of river water and blood. He turned away.

Like an entire town had looked away when she'd gone missing.

As one of the local foster-child transplants, Julie had been assumed a runaway when she had vanished. Justin had missed her more than her caseworker and guardian combined.

But why here? Why now? Was there truth to waking the dead?

He had no time to answer his thoughts. He had no time to beg her forgiveness. Her filthy hair flew about as if a wind had suddenly kicked up. Her arms shot out from her sides as if she prepared to hug him. And her eye and partner socket grew wide.

"Run." Her voice rasped across destroyed vocal cords. "Run, Justin!"

He scrambled to his feet and sprinted toward the railroad tracks, believing that once off the field he'd be safe. He didn't know if he ran from Julie or from something she saw that he didn't, or couldn't—and it didn't matter.

As he left the field, crossed the tracks and kept running toward his house, he realized he'd been running for months. His whole family had been—his mother dragging him across the country to escape the memory that had followed them. And he wondered how long he'd be running from Julie, and the guilt of not answering that last text message the day she had disappeared.

Calling the Dead

Matt Venne
RICHARD DAWSON AND THE FAMILY FEUD PHANTASMS

MATT VENNE is the screenwriter of *White Noise 2*, the upcoming *Rambo 5: John Rambo* and *Mirrors 2*, and wrote the teleplays for the Masters Of Horror episode entitled *Pelts* (directed by Dario Argento), and the Fear Itself episode entitled *Spooked* (directed by Brad Anderson). His first book, *Cruel Summer*, was recently published by Tasmaniac Publications, and his first comic book, *Beyond The Wall*, is being published by IDW in October of 2009 as a four-issue limited series. He lives in Los Angeles with his wife, Brynna, and their two daughters.

January 07, 1865. West Virginia. Richard Dawson, host of *The Family Feud*, sprinted naked through the Appalachian Mountains of yore, the Devil snapping at his heels, panting furiously, confused, brambles ripping the flesh of his arms as he tripped and fell down a thorny hillside, crashing into a twisted heap at the bottom.

He looked around, discovered he was lying at the mouth of a dark cave.

He looked over his shoulder, to the top of the hill.

The Tall Old Man appeared at its crest, looking down into the darkness below for his prey, eyes rimmed with anger in the moonlit darkness. The Tall Old Man had a beard that grew in thick tangles, his dark flannel suit in the style worn by preachers in the mid-1800s, his skin sallow from too much moonshine and backwoods darkness.

Richard Dawson kept still and managed to hold his breath, even as he began to feel the rabid tickle of myriad insects crawling along his naked flesh. Dawson glanced down, discovered he was covered in a sea of bulbous red ants. . . The Tall Old Man took a deep whiff of the midnight sky, filling his nostrils with all the scents of his backwoods lands, seemed to trace the smell of the ants—his ants, Dawson somehow knew—to their source: The Tall Old Man's angry gaze landed upon Richard Dawson as he raised his heavy pinewood cane and commanded, "Give me the answers I seek!"

Dawson trembled at the dark mouth of the cave, seemingly pinned beneath the Tall Old Man's paralyzing gaze, a meek groaning now echoing from the darkness within the cave. . .

The Tall Old Man cried out again, louder this time: "Give me the answers!"

Dawson struggled against the blanket of red ants as they crawled across every inch of his body, thought about telling the Tall Old Man what he wanted to hear, but held fast in his silence: Richard Dawson was many things—mindless 1970s game show host, heavy drinker, chain smoker, serial womanizer, maybe even a bit of a bastard if he did say so himself—but he was not a crook. And in a life filled with too many shades of gray morality, Richard Dawson clung dearly to those aspects of himself that were beyond reproach. He had not, nor would he ever, help a contestant win *The Family Feud* by slipping him or her the answers, even if it was a hellhound hillbilly in the midst of the Appalachian mountains who was hunting him down through some nightmare landscape.

Richard Dawson looked back up at the Tall Old Man, yelled, "Survey says!" then flipped him the bird before scampering into the mouth of the cave. The meek groaning grew louder, but somehow Dawson felt compelled to follow the enigmatic sound. . . made his way around several twists and turns. . . fumbling through the darkness. . . stopped in terror upon discovering the source of the sound.

A young man wearing a Union Army soldier's uniform stood by himself in the center of the cave, confused and unaware that Richard Dawson was watching him. As blood began to dribble out from his Union Army cap, the young man removed the cap and wrung it out, blood spilling from the cap as if it was an overstuffed sponge, the young man oblivious to the fact that his head had been smashed in with a rock, his skull shattered, his brain exposed and bleeding black bile. The young man put his cap back on, but it quickly soaked up more blood from his fatal wound, whereupon he wrung it out all over again. . . .

As the young man turned, he and Dawson made eye contact, the young man startled by Dawson's presence, Dawson noticing that the young man's uniform was stenciled with the faded words *McCOY, ASA HARMAN*.

The young man held Richard Dawson's gaze a moment longer, the blood pouring from his bludgeoned skull. . . finally implored, "Please don't let the godforsaken Hatfields win this thing. . . please. . . please. . .

Just tell us what the survey says."

Richard Dawson shook his head.

Anger lashed at the young man's features. He advanced toward Dawson, fingers wringing every last drop of blood from his Union cap, teeth grit in stubborn rage, blood pulsing from his battered brain as he opened his mouth too wide and the sound of a Family Feud *STRIKE!* signifying a wrong answer echoed throughout the darkness of the cave...

* * *

March 18, 1979. Hollywood, CA. Richard Dawson awoke from the nightmare on the floor of his on-the-lot office, sun prying into the darkness through slivers between the Venetian blinds, brain sludgy with moonshine, trying to get his heavy legs to carry him to the bathroom before he puked all over the new hardwood floors.

Stumbling across his lavish office, he knocked over a couple Emmy Awards and his favorite photograph of him and Bob Crane from their *Hogan's Heroes* days. . . . Finally made it to his private bathroom, fell to his knees and lifted the toilet seat just in time to purge himself with several moments of violent retching. . . .

Having the descendants of the Hatfield and McCoy clans for a special episode of *The Family Feud* seemed like a good idea several months back, but now, stuck in the thick of all their madness and country superstitions, Dawson couldn't wait to get those hillbillies back on a plane and out of his life forever.

Of course, Dawson being Dawson, he'd gotten himself into this mess: he'd taken one look at the young McCoy girl, Constance, when both families arrived on the lot yesterday, and decided his presence would be needed at all the walk-through rehearsals and hospitality parties leading up to this afternoon's taping of the show.

But now, praying to the porcelain god in nothing but last night's dirty boxer shorts and a pair of dress socks, Richard Dawson had once again come to regret the error of his philandering ways.

Dawson's warm thoughts about last night's glories with Constance McCoy were suddenly ripped from his head, Dawson staring dumbstruck, still on his knees, arms wrapped around the toilet. Streams of red ants were crawling out from the pulpy mess he vomited into the toilet bowl, all of the insects covered in a sheen of stomach bile, as if they'd been expulsed from Dawson's own soft belly.

Dawson's stomach turned at the sight.

He faced the bathroom mirror.

Began to wash the sweat from his face, frowned in mute revulsion.

One last red ant straggled out from between his lips. . . then stopped, perched on Dawson's bloated cheek, staring at their reflection in the mirror.

As if studying Dawson. With reproach.

And then, as if the words were pulled from the depths of his belly, Dawson suddenly blurted out, *"Devil ants!"*

The lone red ant almost seemed to nod as it continued on its way at that, Dawson watching in still-drunken disbelief as the insect crawled purposefully down his neck. . . his chest. . . his belly. . . his leg. . . finally making its way across the bathroom floor until it was reunited with its clan, whereupon Dawson discovered that the sea of red ants that he'd puked-up had now formed themselves into one single pulsing entity, Dawson staring wide-eyed at the sight of their two-word insectoid slogan:

DEVILANSE

Dawson absently repeated his earlier phrase in disbelief—*"Devil ants"*—as he got on all fours to examine the red ants more closely, poking at them with a shaky finger. He yelped when one of them bit him, began sucking at the wound as there was a knock at his office door, followed by a P.A. meekly informing him, "You're wanted on-set in an hour, Mister Dawson. Just a reminder."

"Yeah, yeah, I'll be there when I get there, kid," Dawson shot back, still staring at the sea of ants on the bathroom floor as he heard the P.A.'s footsteps scurry away down the hall back toward Stage 54. Dawson got to his feet, realized he needed to get dressed for hair and make-up soon, absently glancing at the bite mark on his finger.

Pulpy black dribbles of infected-looking blood trickled from the wound.

"That doesn't look like an ant bite," Dawson muttered, but before he could give it any more thought he suddenly began smearing the sick blood across his office's bathroom walls, as if possessed by some other force, the black blood flowing down through the ages like ink from a permanent marker, dark and thick, Dawson writing in an automatic frenzy, then collapsing to floor once finished, more tired than he'd ever been, staring at the walls, aghast at what he'd scribbled with his own insect-infected blood:

TELLDEVILANSE

"I'm going crazy!" Dawson said. "Finally going bat guano crazy, trying to get myself to talk to a bunch of red ants!"

And for some reason this brought a smile to the game show host's face. All the days and nights of drinking his way through the inanities of hosting a mindless game show, all the kisses on the lips of the female contestants in his fight against an increasingly politically correct viewership, all the herpes tests and STDs from days and nights of "private rehearsals," all the hundreds of millions of times he'd uttered the phrase: "Survey says!" All of it was finally catching up with him. After all, Dawson reasoned, a man can only reduce himself to an avatar of the lowest common denominator for so long before his soul finally crumbles under the weight of its own emptiness, no matter how much it paid.

Dawson got up to splash some water on his face, looked in the mirror, gasped in startled fright.

The Tall Old Man from his nightmare was looking back at him, the same crazy, moonshine-addled smile pulling at his bearded cheeks as he commanded, "Tell me what the survey says. You owe it to the Hatfields. You owe it to us!"

Dawson took a swipe at the bathroom mirror, shattering it into numerous pieces of broken reflective glass, numerous Richard Dawsons staring back at him now, cutting his knuckles in the process. Now the crew would really start talking, thought Dawson, as he grabbed a roll of toilet paper and wrapped his knuckles to stop the bleeding. "Punched his own reflection in the mirror after an all-night binge," he could imagine them whispering behind his back on set.

Dawson scowled, angry at the voices in his head as he bent down to pick up the broken shards of mirror. He noticed the slogan he'd written with his own blood—TELL DEVIL ANSE—reflected numerous times back at him, and something clicked: "It's not about the... red ants. Devil Ants is somebody's... *name*."

* * *

The security guard at the ABC Television Center had seen Richard Dawson do a lot of strange things in the six years he'd been working the front gate, so the sight of the game show host racing his brand new 1979 Jaguar off the lot wearing nothing but his boxer shorts, a T-shirt, and slippers hardly elicited a shrug... Nor did the sight of Dawson returning to the lot, Jaguar now filled with library books.

* * *

Richard Dawson stared at the vintage photograph inside the library book he'd checked out. The Tall Old Man from his nightmares was, as he'd begun to suspect, William Anderson "Devil Anse" Hatfield, and the young man in the Union Solder Civil War uniform was Asa Harman

McCoy.

Dawson shook his head... almost marveling. Here were the two men with whom America's great family feud—its original family feud—had begun: Devil Anse Hatfield and Asa Harman McCoy.

As Dawson continued to read through the books he'd checked out about the history of the Hatfield-McCoy Family Feud. He discovered that it had officially begun when Asa Harman McCoy was killed by Devil Anse Hatfield and his crew in a cave somewhere near where the Appalachian Trail now passes. From that moment of bloodshed, two families were put on a warpath of Shakespearean proportions that lasted nearly two decades, and would forever be a part of American lore.

Richard Dawson shook his head as he realized he'd become a pawn in this most famous of American feuds. Although he couldn't care less about history or politics or Union versus Confederate soldiers or bootlegging or whatever else those hicks of yore cared about, there was one thing Richard Dawson did care about: Richard Dawson. And there was no way he was going to let some pack of hillbilly ghosts take a piss on him and his game show. Ratings were through the roof, and phantoms or no phantoms, Dawson wasn't about to watch everything slip away in a sea of accusations about his show being rigged.

Richard Dawson defiantly swept the library books from the table, took a big pull from the bottle of moonshine that hot little Constance McCoy had brought by his office late last night, got dressed in his best suit, put on his favorite pinky ring—took another hearty swig of the moonshine... and then another... and then one more for good measure—then headed out to make the magic happen. It was time to host a game show, and Richard Dawson wasn't gonna be pushed around by anyone, ghosts of the Hatfield-McCoy Clan or otherwise!

* * *

That afternoon's taping of the Hatfields versus McCoys *Family Feud* special went off without too much of a hitch: Richard Dawson lip-locked every female contestant on both sides of the great American family divide with extra vigor, even did a little tongue wrestling with Constance McCoy to the studio audience's delight, and nearing the end of the afternoon's festivities the score was very close, the McCoys only trailing the Hatfields by ten points to see which family could claim victory in America's ultimate courtroom: the boob tube.

One more segment to tape. During the commercial break before the final round, Richard Dawson looked out into the studio audience from his perch backstage. Although he'd been playing it cool, he was still worried about what might happen. His hands were shaking, and he needed an additional scotch on top of his usual two-per-break to make it through. But as Dawson lit his cigarette, his eyes on the crowd, his scotch fell from nerveless fingers.

Devil Anse Hatfield sat in the front row, eyes locked intently on Richard Dawson, the Tall Old Man looking even more ghastly due to the white hot stage lights he was seated beneath. Devil Anse's long tangled beard appeared to be. . . moving – and it wasn't until Dawson looked more closely that he realized Devil Anse's beard was comprised entirely of bulbous red ants, furiously crawling all over one another.

Devil Anse smiled at Richard Dawson, his rotten vocal chords guttural in their pleas that only Dawson could hear: "Tell me what the survey says!"

Richard Dawson instinctively backed away as two P.A.s swooped down to clean up the broken glass from his spilled drink. Dawson bumped into another young production assistant, turning to apologize, only to flinch upon discovering he was staring into the dead eyes of Asa Harman McCoy, who clutched Dawson's arm tightly, blood dribbling from beneath his Union Soldier's cap as he, too, begged, "Tell me what the survey says!"

Richard Dawson looked away from the phantasms of the age-old family feud, made eye contact with all their living descendants gathered on stage, all of them hopeful that he would take a stand and help settle the matter once and for all. . . but Richard Dawson just scowled, waved his hands at the horrors all around him, causing them to dissipate into nothingness as he stormed the stage, signaled he was ready to go, commanding, "Roll tape. We got a game show to shoot!"

* * *

By night's end, Richard Dawson was so blasted on highballs, he couldn't even remember which family had ended up winning, and he didn't care, either. All Richard Dawson knew was that to thine own self he'd been true, always had been, always would be. That was just the way Richard Dawson rolled, ancient American ghosts of the Mountain State messing with him or not. In the end, it didn't matter if the Hatfields or McCoys won; their backwoods feud had been as mindless as Dawson's syndicated one, only they didn't have the 3.5 million dollars a year to show for it that Dawson did.

Dawson laughed at the hillbillys' backwoods ignorance as he unzipped his fly to take a piss in his office bathroom... realized all the day's excitement had gotten his engines a bit revved up, so to speak... wondered if that hot little Constance McCoy was still up at the Sheraton, and if so, he thought hopefully, maybe she'd be up for a bit of the ol' Dawson Mambo.

Richard Dawson's mind froze. Terror trickled down his spine in time with the urine that dribbled down his leg, his wide eyes locked gripped by the trail of red ants that he'd just noticed crawling around his feet....

Searching Richard Dawson out...

On behalf of the Tall Old Man, whose silhouetted footsteps could now be seen in the crack at the bottom of the bathroom door. Devil Anse's guttural old voice scratching at Dawson's psyche: "Survey says..."

Douglas F. Warrick
HER FATHER'S COLLECTION

DOUGLAS F. WARRICK is a writer and an editor. His stories have appeared in *Apex Digest*, *Murky Depths*, and online at Pseudopod.org. The anthology he coedited with his frequent collaborator Kyle S. Johnson, a book of short stories inspired by Nick Cave songs called *Up Jumped the Devil*, is due out from PS Publishing next year. This story would never have happened without the cooperation of the kind folks at the FCA law firm, the staff responsible for the carriage trail's upkeep, the endlessly patient employees of Charleston's city hall, and Doug's ever enthusiastic father, Don, who offered his invaluable (and free) services as a research assistant. Doug lives in Dayton, Ohio, with his wife. Visit him at www.douglasfwarrick.com.

She runs. Oh, yes, she runs. Her bare feet slap like hands against the rough loose-packed dirt of her father's carriage trail. Tiny rocks stick to her heels, gnawing little divots into them, little pink craters like bite marks, and why yes, that does seem just about right, doesn't it? Because Sunrise Mansion does have teeth. Sunrise Mansion devours.

She can hear the severe and shrill laughter of the Girls, and she feels like she has missed the set-up and punch-line of a particularly cruel joke.

Somewhere up above her, in her father's awful house, there is a fireplace. She feels the meanness and the promise of it, even though seventy years have passed since she has seen it in person, seventy years since she died. Her sides hurt and her lungs blaze white-hot in her chest, and all she wants to think about is the run, the dash, the great blind escape. Despite all of this, her father's fireplace crawls up out of her memory and its image glows inside her head. The faces that stretch and strain from its surface, each one a stolen thing, a collection of sculpted Christs and gargoyle heads, each from a different place and a different time. The stones set into the face of the mantle, each with its birthplace carved into the surface. Westminster Abbey. The Birthplace of William the Conqueror. The Great Wall of China.

Some part of her thinks, *My daddy collects stolen ghosts.*

The dress. The dress keeps tangling around her ankles and she keeps tripping, almost falling. Oh, her daddy gave her this dress, didn't he? Oh, yes, he did. He gave her this dress and…

And he says, "Isabelle, love. The pictures tonight?"

And they go. He in his white suit with wax in his mustache and she in her fine new dress. God, how pretty she looks! And she never thinks so, never ever, but tonight with her handsome daddy smiling beside her, she feels perfectly gorgeous. They park the car on the street and when they get out, someone walks up and shakes her daddy's hand and says, "Good to see you, Mr. Governor," even though Daddy hasn't been Governor for decades. Everything shines. That joy she feels, that pride. . . God, it leaps from her and wraps itself around everything! They watch

The Black Pirate with Douglas Fairbanks. It is in Technicolor. In the dark next to her father, in his white suit with his pipe-stem sticking out of his vest pocket, everything in the whole wide world is painted in those colors.

On the way home, her father runs the car into a tree. And something sharp hits her hard in the forehead. And all the color drowns in itself. And everything is no color at all.

She tries not to cry. That was the subtle clutch of his big thick fingers around her ankle, so light that she didn't even notice. It kept her next to him, even at thirty-five years old, old enough to be married, to go dancing, to experience all the wonderful things the world had to offer. Damn her daddy.

She rounds a corner and sees the Girls standing in the middle of the trail and holding hands. They shift. Always. Their bodies can't decide how they died. Now their necks are swollen and stretched and purple, and their heads twist away at strange angles and the blood vessels in their eyes have burst. Now their beautiful dresses, the elaborate Charleston Civil War chic they must have affected so well while they breathed, shred in a dozen places, fill with charred bullet holes, and their faces and their arms are pocked with the same, each dry and black and burnt around the edges, like open unblinking eyes. It's the power of the living tongue, of what people say about the dead. They say the Girls were hanged. They say they died by firing squad.

It changes you after a while.

Isabelle shudders, and the Girls smile. Daddy's voice dances through her head and she is swallowed by memory again. What had he said? In front of that great Frankenstein mantle? He had said...

"Do you know what happened to them?" he says, with his shirt open at the chest and his vest unbuttoned, sitting in his big leather chair in front of the fireplace. She is six... maybe seven when Daddy finds the bodies. While the crew built the carriage trail through the wide and winding woods up the hill to Sunrise. Two bodies, mummified and buried. And Daddy reburies them, sets up a stone to mark their resting place. Now in the sitting room, he tilts his glass from side to side, watches the gin slide from edge to edge. "Spies, darling. Spies for the Union. Can you believe it? Tried and executed. Right here."

It is a week, maybe two, after they found them, and Daddy looks so tired.

She hadn't understood then, just a little girl, no real scars to compare to those of her father. But there was something else there, wasn't there? Yes, something shameful and secret and warm kept all to himself. Her father's vice. Stolen ghosts.

So it began with the Girls.

Now the Girls nod to Isabelle. And no, no, no, she does not want to go to them, does not want to walk within whispering distance, where she can't tell which of them is doing the whispering, but yes, yes, yes, her feet move her forward, and now there is a Girl on either side of Isabelle, both dead and shifting.

"The key," says one of the girls.

"Oh, yes, the key," says the other.

They giggle together.

She tries so hard not to let her skin go thick with gooseflesh as their whispers wash over her. She fails. She tells them she knows. They need the key.

There is a door set into the mantle of that terrible fireplace, that massive golem in her father's house. A tiny tin door with a keyhole set in its center.

The Girls giggle again. There's nothing nice about that sound. There is only something final. Because the Girls call the shots. They always have, ever since the crash and the death and the night she woke up as a part of her father's ghost collection. Making plans, giving orders, whispering, "Run, Isabelle! Run for Sunrise!" so loud that indeed she had to run, if only to get away from their choked baby-doll voices. "Get us out," they whispered (and still whisper). "You can get us out."

So she runs. Like she has run every night since the last one of her life.

When she sees the house sliding over the horizon, the first tears come and she almost stops. Almost. Too angry and sad and dead to do that. So she hikes up that beautiful dress and clutches at the hem in one tight white fist and keeps running.

Damn her daddy and the memories that keep pushing up into her head, her father with his hands on the wheel, it was hot in the car, the kind of summer night in Charleston that would melt. . .

It is the kind of summer night in Charleston that melts the wax her daddy puts in his mustache, and now, with his fists locked around the steering wheel, her daddy's mustache is drooping. She can see the first beads of wet wax work their way down like vines and it makes her laugh like a little girl. Thirty-five years old and laughing like a little girl. She tells him she loves him. He smiles and says, "I love you too, Izza. You're my baby girl."

But Daddy looks sad, so sad, and she reaches over and puts her hand on his arm. And she asks her big beautiful daddy what's wrong.

"Going to leave me, darling. Past time. Pretty young woman like you."

And she tells him, no, Daddy, no, not yet, she's not going anywhere just yet, but he lets loose one tight fist and waves her away.

"I know better," he says, and the first drops of wax slip away and pad against the thigh of his white pants. Her daddy's eyes are so wide tonight. So wide it scares her. They stare forward, no twitching, no blinking, and he drives like a man piloting a bullet.

They ride up onto the hill, toward the carriage trail and home. She puts her hand on his leg, over the place where the wax dripped, and catches the next few spatters. They are quiet.

And when her daddy says, "The only way to keep something forever," she's hardly listening anymore. Just breathing in the night, and swallowing the sounds. She doesn't really hear him until he says, "Is losing it for good," and jerks the steering wheel sideways. He has time to say, "Sorry, baby girl."

She runs. She runs past the monument he built for her out here, the anchor he tied to her. The stone Madonna is gone, lifted up by the root, but her ashes are in there somewhere, and she shivers and knows that she should not be in two places at once. She runs up the old stone steps, slick and made green with age and mildew.

She does not stop running until her bare feet slide onto the cold stone of the porch. Has she come this far before? She can't remember. She doesn't think so. No time. No time.

The Girls are here, holding hands and sharing secrets. Shot. Hanged. Both. They wave, and Isabelle grinds her teeth against her tongue and screws her eyes shut and pretends they are not here. Still, they whisper. They say, "The key, baby girl." Isabelle wants to scream.

She opens the door. And the three of them go in together. Sunrise Mansion breathes them in, and they are swallowed when the Girls close the door. The front hall is too long, longer than it ever was when she lived, and lined with her father's things. The ghastly old collection. Things once owned by the dead, and now owned by them again. And framed in the doorway to the sitting room, the cloister of the slippery-sick fireplace with its many faces, is her daddy. He stands with his back to them, his hands clasped behind him, in his white Mark Twain suit. He breathes, or he seems to. And Isabelle is split in two. She loves him. She hates him. She blames and forgives and reconvicts and once again pardons him.

There is noise. There is so very much noise! Just looking at him, standing there and pretending not to know that they have intruded into this place, her world is filled with sound, crashing sound, crunching sound, metal on metal on glass on dirt on flesh crash crunch scream she should scream she can't scream because she does not have a voice has never had a voice sound!

She is on her knees with the heels of her hands pressed to her ears before she knows she has fallen. And still her father will not lower his chin and crane his neck to see her. Behind her, the Girls lick their lips and hiss like snake-harlots, and all that noise still presses down on her, paralyzes her.

Her father says, "So good to see you, baby girl. You look splendid." And the noise breaks. Silence fills the cracks, shuttles the sound away.

So Isabelle stands. With shaky knees, with her pretty dress tangling around her bare ankles. She steps forward. And she sees the fireplace beyond her poor awful daddy.

Oh, no, no, no.

All of the faces are gone. The faces of Christ and the faces of a thousand nameless under-bit gargoyles and goblins. All sucked in and away. And in their place now, staring out with sadness set in chiseled eyes, her daddy's face stares back a thousand times. She thinks, *Don't turn around now, Daddy. God, please, don't turn around.* She does not want to know what her handsome daddy has become, does not want to see the swirling vertigo where Sunrise has stolen her daddy's face.

He stays put. His hands remain clasped. The faces in the fireplace close their eyes and grit their teeth. "I didn't mean a thing but love, Izza. You know that."

And she does. Because the only way to keep something forever is to lose it for good. But it hurts. And she's too tired to fight the tears.

The Girls slide up on either side of her and she winces at the smell of breath from lungs that no longer breathe. They say, "The key?"

And she nods.

Her daddy's sad stone faces, they all curl up on themselves like the faces of crying men, and they say, "Baby girl, I am so sorry."

His body reaches into his front vest pocket, where he always kept his beautiful Meerschaum pipe, and he pulls out the thing she wants. The key. Oh, the key!

She reaches over his shoulder and snatches it, and close up like this, she sees the place where his face should be. Just a glance. Just a glimmer in her periphery. But, oh it is awful. And she begins to cry so hard that she almost makes a noise.

The Girls push her forward, past the faceless thing shaped like her father, out of the front hall and into the sitting room. Toward the fireplace, that wall of faces that used to be stolen and are now all her father's. Those stones once carved with their birthplaces, each to a one now reads SUNRISE.

And there is the door. The tiny tin door with the keyhole in its center.

Her father's faces say, "There's nothing behind that door. But you know that, baby girl. This never ends."

"The key!" whisper the Girls. And they drown her poor daddy into silence.

She unlocks the door. And she opens it. And now, oh yes, now she. . .

She runs. Oh, yes, she runs. Her bare feet slap like hands against the rough loose-packed dirt of her father's carriage trail. Tiny rocks stick to her heels, gnawing little divots into them, little pink craters like bite marks, and why yes, that does seem just about right, doesn't it? Because Sunrise Mansion does have teeth. Sunrise Mansion devours.

She can hear the severe and shrill laughter of the Girls, and she feels like she has missed the set-up and punch-line of a particularly cruel joke.

Steve Vernon
WHERE YOU GONNA RUN TO?

STEVE VERNON learned the storytelling tradition from his grandfather. He now teaches the art to Nova Scotia school children. He is the author of nearly one hundred published short stories as well as the ghost story collections *Haunted Harbours, Wicked Woods and Halifax Haunts* (Nimbus Publishing), as well as an upcoming children's picture book on the sea monsters and wood beasts of the maritimes, *Maritime Monsters*. Steve lives in Halifax and his heart still hammers to the beat of steel.

Fear tastes of old pennies, sweat and sawdust.

Waylon ran through the darkness, his heart hammering like a thunder of drums. He hadn't gone home because he knew full well that would be the very first place the police would look for him.

Why had he done it?

He'd lost his temper. That was plain enough. Not that he'd ever loved that job in the hardwood flooring factory, but knowing he and five other men had lost their jobs because of that new computerized saw hit him harder than it ought to. Sure, they could blame it on the economy if they wanted to. They could blame it on safety and speed of production too. They could even blame it on Waylon's drinking.

But he hadn't been drunk when he was fired.

He could still see the foreman Roscoe Huntington standing with his big fat moon-face all greasy with sweat. Roscoe had looked down at his feet, like he was ashamed and he ought to have been. He'd tried to pretend he was apologizing to Waylon for handing him that pink slip.

And then somehow like magic that ball peen hammer had been in Waylon's fist as he'd swung that high hard arc landing smack-dab solid against Roscoe's receding hairline.

Who'd have thought a skull would have been so easy to crack?

Waylon had headed for the fire exit, slamming the door open and the fire alarm had gone off and people stood in that deer-in-the-headlights way that most folks had in times of crisis and no one knew what to do—except Waylon.

Waylon had run.

Sinner man, where you gonna run to?

He could hear that old folk song his daddy used to sing to him haunting him as he ran—that old song that went on and on about running to the rocks and running to the river and running to the moon without ever finding salvation.

That was really all Waylon's daddy had been good for—singing old songs that no one cared to hear anymore.

The old man hadn't even sung on key.

Waylon ran through the back lot of the factory, up over the pallets that teetered against the storm wire fence and then into the woods, his work boots pounding up clouds of summer-dried dust behind him.

He ran like he had a compass in his feet.

He knew this country.

He'd been born and raised and had played here when he was a kid.

From the woods he made his way into the hills and finally found himself kneeling at the mouth of the Big Bend Tunnel, just wishing for a cool drink of water.

I run to the rock, cried rock won't you hide me.

They'll never think to look for me here, he thought. Nobody came here anymore except for the occasional tourist, and he would find few here this late in the day.

All he had to do was get through the tunnel and keep on walking.

Nobody would find him.

Only he couldn't remember this old tunnel being so dark as it was. He should have brought himself a light. He made a mental note to himself: the next time he murdered his foreman in a fit of rage he should be sure to bring along a flashlight.

Only he didn't have a flashlight. All that he had was the ball peen hammer. He couldn't figure out just why he hadn't dropped it, but there it was, hanging in his hand like it would stick there until judgement day.

I might as well hang on to it, he thought to himself. There was no telling what might be lurking in this tunnel that burrowed beneath the mighty Allegheney Mountains.

He stepped forward.

His feet sank into a foot of cold standing water. The early spring rain had flooded the tunnel. He stepped a little further. Now that he was into the darkness he could see a layer of mist rising up from the standing water.

I run to the river, but the river was bleeding.

His work boots weren't made for wading any more than they were made for running, but he told himself he could handle the discomfort. Maybe he couldn't handle working at the factory. He definitely hadn't handled being fired very well.

But he could put up with a mile of soggy walking.

Who knows? If those West Virginia police bring along a pack of hunting hounds, the water might throw them off the track. Of course, if the hounds lead the police to the tunnel mouth it wouldn't take too much shrewd deductive thinking to figure out just where Waylon went to. They'd hunt him down and drag him to the judge who would bang his gavel and before you could say hammer-time Waylon would be spending his days and nights in Alderson Prison.

Never mind that.

Don't think about that now.

Just keep walking.

He waded in a little further and then he heard something in the darkness. Something ringing.

KLING!

"Oh my hammer," a voice sang out, strong and low.

KLING!

"Hammer, ring."

KLING!

He wasn't alone.

"Oh, my hammer."

KLING!

"Hammer, ring."

Whoever it was they were further down the tunnel. That left Waylon only two choices. He could turn back and risk running into the town police or move further into the tunnel and confront whoever was singing.

KLING!

Well, whatever was making that ringing noise, it sure didn't sound much like a manhunt to Waylon.

"Oh, my hammer."

It sounded like somebody working.

If this was a story, Waylon would have followed the sound, but this wasn't a story—this was a dirty old tunnel through crumbling West Virginia shale. Waylon had no way to go but straight ahead, towards the ringing and the singing.

KLING!

He tried to count his paces but lost his count somewhere in the darkness. Instead, he found himself counting the ringing sounds. He had been walking for about one hundred and twenty-eight rings when he saw the figure in the darkness.

"Hammer, ring."

KLING!

One hundred twenty-nine.

Big wasn't big enough a word for this man. The figure standing in front of Waylon was a mountain of a man, swinging a sledge hammer that looked heavy enough to give Godzilla a goose egg without half-trying.

"Oh, my hammer."

The man's voice was low and soulful, as if he were singing from about six feet below the soles of his work boots.

"Hammer, ring."

KLING!

When that hammer hit home sparks were raised and a glow seemed to pervade the tunnel darkness. The hammer-glow built like cinder raising the ashes of a long dead fire.

Waylon could see the big man clearly now. The man's arms looked like they were made out of anaconda and anchor chains. The muscles in his back moved and rolled like mountains of jet. His back was as wide as the sledge handle was long. His shoulder blades looked like he was wearing bowling balls for shoulder pads.

And then the big man turned around and smiled.

"Oh there you are," he said in a voice that rolled out like black strap molasses. "I was wondering what was keeping you."

Waylon knew he ought to keep on running but there was something downright compelling about finding this man hammering deep down in the darkness.

"What are you digging for?" Waylon asked.

"I'm digging for my life and anything that comes after," the big man said. "This is what I do."

"You dig in an abandoned tunnel?"

"I dig because this is how I was born. With a hammer in my hand and a song in my throat."

Great, Waylon thought. I'm running from the law and I run into a tone-deaf blacksmith.

"Say, look here," the big man said.

He spread the palm of his big right hand out before Waylon.

"I'm not a palm reader," Waylon protested. "Whatever you're trying to sell me, there's no deal."

But Waylon couldn't look away.

"I don't need a palm reader," the big man said, dropping each word like a wish on the back of a penny dropped into the mouth of a bottomless wishing well. "A witch woman in the Black River area looked in my hand and told me straight."

Waylon kept staring at the big man's hand. He swore he could see a railroad track and a tunnel and a forever long snake twisting across the plain of the palm.

"That old witch woman, she told me that I would hammer my heart out in the belly of the Big Bend Tunnel. She told me that I would hammer me down a steam engine and that when that steam engine had quit and died that I would hammer six more feet down and lay there in the dirt and let the years and darkness and song cover over me."

Waylon saw ridges and valleys and mountains and shadow breaking and looming across that big man's hands.

"She told me that men and women would sing of my work and that even after I was dead and gone that I would work in the darkness of this mountain until another man came along carrying a hammer marked with murdered blood."

Waylon felt the weight of that ball peen hammer still hanging like a piece of gallow-bait, dangling in his left hand.

"You put the murdering hammer down here in the dirt and pick up my hammer," the big man said. "You got a lifetime of sinning to hammer out."

Waylon looked at the big man's hammer. To his eyes it looked like a boxcar mounted on a telephone pole.

"There's no way I can use that hammer," Waylon protested.

And yet the ball peen that he had buried in Roscoe Huntington's forehead slid from the grip of his left hand like a greased serpent sliding through a dead man's hand.

"You bear the mark the same as me," the big man said. "Right there on your palms."

Waylon looked at his hands. All he could see were the wide staring eyes of Roscoe Huntington staring back at him.

And behind those eyes the eyes of his dad.

"Pick that hammer up," the big man ordered.

Waylon bent and took up the big man's hammer.

"Swing it," the big man said. "Swing it like you were born to."

Waylon leaned and twisted back, and that big man's hammer seemed to leap up and swing down.

KLING!

"And sing," the big man said. "Sing like you mean to."

"Oh, my hammer," Waylon sung as the hammer swung.

KLING!

"Hammer, ring."

He found he took to the rhythm of the hammer as if he were born to it.

"You not the first," the big man said as Waylon worked away. "Neither was I. But you be the second last born. There'll be another come down this tunnel, by and by. You wait for him and see."

Waylon kept singing.

The hammer kept on swinging.

"The next one come down here will be the one you're waiting for," the big man said. "He'll take up your hammer, and you'll go home."

"I can't go home," Waylon said, as he swung the hammer up.

"We all go home, sooner or later," the big man said. "Just look for the next man."

KLING!

"How will I know him?" Waylon asked.

"Same as I knew you," the big man said. "By the marks on his palms."

And then the big man turned and walked into the darkness of the tunnel, seeming to rise up like a fistful of smoke through the brickwork and the shale and the shadows beyond.

KLING!

And as the big man rose away Waylon could hear him sing a song—soft, sad and slow.

"John Henry said to his daddy, I believe it's my time to go, just lay my hammer in the shadow of the hole and up to the mountain I will go, lordy, lordy, up to the mountain I will go."

Waylon kept on hammering for as long as it took.

Fran Friel
THE ROSE GHOST OF RAVENSWOOD

FRAN FRIEL is a two-time Bram Stoker finalist and winner of the Black Quill Award. She writes horror, dark fantasy and science fiction at the beach in coastal New England, and like all "respectable" authors, she is currently working on a novel. Look for Fran's award-winning collection, *Mama's Boy and Other Dark Tales*, at ApexBookCompany.com, and stop by for a chat at facebook and her blogs—the cyber-door is always open. For more info visit: franfriel.com or franfriel.blogspot.com.

Lynnie Sparrow fussed around the daybed in the living room, gently tucking and smoothing the covers, trying not to disturb the frail old woman. The feel of the quilt made her heart ache—so soft from all the years of Granny Lynn bundling her and Bethy against the cold West Virginia winters.

"Leave her alone. You'll wake her up," said the woman in front of the blaring television. "You come in here, after how many years? Think you can just take over. Typical."

After all this time, her sister's scowling disapproval still withered Lynnie. When their daddy left, Bethy stepped up and took over. The scars ran deep.

Lynnie felt a delicate hand grasp her own in reassurance.

"Hush, Bethy," said the old woman in a raspy voice.

Bethy turned back to her roaring game show, arms folded firmly across her chest.

Along with a *slam* of the back door came a shout, "Granny Lynn, I've got a surprise for you!" The small force of nature that was Olivia Lynn Sparrow flew into the living room, huffing and puffing, full of excitement.

Bethy jumped to her feet, hands on hips. "Can't you control that brat? If you can't, I will."

"I told you to hush, Bethy. Now I might be dying, but I ain't dead yet, so stop acting like we's in the funeral parlor already." With a nearly toothless grin, the old woman turned to the child. "Now what's got you all fired up, little one?"

From behind her back Olivia produced a fat red rose ready to burst into bloom.

"Do you like it, Granny?"

"I love it, child." Granny Lynn took the bud in her shaking hand and breathed in the heady scent. Hesitating for a moment, she asked, "Where did you get this rose, Livvy Lynn?"

"Mister Wilbur gave it to me." The child looked sheepishly over her shoulder at her mother. "Don't worry, mama. He wasn't a stranger. He told me he's an old friend of the family."

Lynnie's face went ashen.

"Now, Lynnie Sparrow, don't you go getting' all upset," said Granny. She turned to the child and continued. "It's one beautiful rose, darlin'. Mister Wilbur sure does know how to grow 'em. He planted those roses a long, long time ago as a weddin' present for his wife, Norma Jean Whitehead. He's been tendin' to 'em like they was precious children ever since."

Trying to remain calm, Lynnie knelt down and gripped her daughter's shoulders. "Listen to me, Livvy. You are not to go near that house again."

"But mama, I promised Mister Wilbur I'd come back to help him. He told me he'd teach me how to—"

"I don't care what he told you. I don't want you anywhere near that house. In fact, I don't want you leaving Granny Lynn's yard. You hear me?"

"But mama—"

"No buts, Olivia Lynn."

The little girl burst into tears and ran outside through the kitchen, slamming the door behind her.

A tear broke the corner of the old woman's eye.

Lynnie sighed. "I'm sorry, Granny."

"No need to be, child. She's just doin' what's natural to her, especially here in Ravenswood. Like your mama, and you and so many of us Sparrow women, she's just following her blood."

"No, Granny. I can't bear to have her suffer like I did. You know it's the only reason I left."

"And you should'a never come back." Her sister nearly spit the words. "You and all your special talents. I was sick to death of them as a child and now I've gotta contend with you *and* your brat seeing things that ain't there. The kid stole that rose and the two of you are indulging her lies."

"Bethy, that's just about enough from you, girl." The old woman broke down into a fit a deep coughing. Lynnie rushed to her side, handing her a clean hankie from the side table.

"Now, see what you done, Lynnie. You gone and upset, Granny. We was fine here 'till you all showed up."

When the old woman regained her breath, she motioned a shaking hand toward Bethy. "Now go on and get supper started, and add a little extra sugar to the sweet tea. You need somethin' to sort out that sour disposition of yours."

Bethy stomped into the kitchen, banging pots, muttering to herself.

"Lynnie, I know why you left and I know you only came home to watch me die, but child, trust an old woman on her death bead, no matter how far away you go, you can't run from what you are." She took a rattling breath and dabbed at the corners of her mouth. "You musta' seen signs with the little one by now. For the sake of both ya'll, you're gonna to have to face the truth."

Lynnie slumped to the side of the bed with her face in her hands. Granny gave her a gentle pat.

"I'm afraid of what will happen to us, Granny. I still have nightmares."

"I know your daddy put you and your mama through hell. But he's gone now. They put him away so he can't hurt nobody no more, so you gotta be strong for that baby girl." The old woman reached for Lynnie's elbow and with surprising strength turned the young woman to face her. "Your mama gave her life to protect you, child, and you gotta step up and protect your own now. Stop runnin' away from what you are. Accept it and help Olivia love what she is—not scared like you been all these years."

At the same moment, the two women felt a faint jolt of intuition and noticed the silence in the kitchen. Lynnie's heart began to race with the horrible thought that occurred to them both.

"Go, child. Hurry."

* * *

"But mama told me not to leave the yard."

"Don't sass me, brat. I'm in charge around here." Bethy dragged the small child down the sidewalk toward the old Whitehead house—the infamous house of the Rose Ghost of Ravenswood. Behind a gap-toothed fence, the crumbling building slumped on its weed choked lot, gray and broken from years of disrepair.

"Now look at this dump. There ain't nothin' but weeds here, so where'd you steal that rose from?"

"I didn't steal it. Mister Wilbur gave it to me."

"Mister Wilbur was dead before I was born, you little liar. Your mother's been fillin' your head with this nonsense just like she tried to do me. She was a liar then and she's a liar now, just like you. Now tell me where you got that rose, or I'm gonna to beat it out of you."

"I got it over there. Right there." She pointed past the fence. "Can't you see?"

Bethy smacked the child across the face. "Liar! Ain't nothin' but weeds."

Hot tears poured down Olivia's cheeks, but her anger at being struck made her bold. She wrenched away from her aunt's grip and pushed through the gate into the garden filled with the velvety blossoms of Mister Wilbur's roses.

"Come back here, brat!" The woman shoved her way past the rickety gate, chasing after Olivia.

"Mister Wilbur," shouted the child.

She wove through the rose bushes, as Bethy chased after her. Bethy's arms were covered in scratches from the cloying weeds, but in her livid pursuit, she barely noticed. Just as she reached out to grab the girl's shoulder, she tripped and hit her forehead on a paving stone. Pulling herself to her knees, she held her bleeding head and looked around, bleary eyed. She was surrounded by a pristine garden filled with lush rose bushes, and standing over her with a shovel raised above his head ready to strike, was an old man in neat blue overalls.

"Stop!" came a voice from across the street. "Please, Mister Wilbur, stop. Don't hurt her." It was Lynnie running toward the Whitehead house.

The man lowered the shovel and stepped back to put his arm

around Olivia's shoulder.

As the blood pulsed from Bethy's forehead, she watched as the image of the old man and his rose bushes faded back into a weed choked yard. She crumpled to the ground, wracked with deep sobs, her patter of tears soaking into the dusty soil.

* * *

The wake for Granny Lynn was an all-day affair. People streamed in and out of the house bringing food and offering stories to Lynnie and her sister about the old woman and how she had touched their lives.

A lady from Granny's church pulled Lynnie aside.

"She never wanted nobody to know, but that gift of your Granny's helped us find Charles when he got lost huntin' in a snowstorm. He'd a froze to death without her." She gave Lynnie a big hug and walked away, dabbing her tears with a tissue.

Lynnie sat down on the sofa beside an older gentleman. She needed a moment to rest her feet. It had been a long week of preparations for the funeral, and she hadn't had time to think about what had happened in the Whitehouse garden the day Granny Lynn passed away.

"Miss Lynn was a blessing," said the gentleman beside her. He leaned close, speaking in a confidential tone. "I went through a real rough patch back when my Lilly died. Don't tell anybody I said this, but I was getting ready to do myself in, and out of the blue the phone rang. I didn't answer, but it started ringing again. It finally annoyed me so much for interrupting my plans, I picked it up. It was your Granny," he said, smiling. "She said she was thinking of me and thought I might like to come over for supper. She wouldn't take no for an answer. I put my gun away and that evening I had the best fried chicken I'd ever eaten." He chuckled to himself and looked up toward the ceiling. "I sure hope my Lilly ain't listening—her chicken was darn good, too."

The old gentleman shook Lynnie's hand and gave her a peck on the cheek. "By the way, even though you moved away, your Granny never stopped talking about you. She said you were really something special. If you're anything like Miss Lynn, I can surely believe it."

* * *

The house was quiet as the last of the visitors departed and the neighbors who had helped clean up had gone home. Lynnie tucked Olivia into bed, and gave the sleepy child a kiss on the forehead. After she turned out the light, she smoothed the soft hair back away from her daughter's face.

"Oh, my little Livvy, Granny was right. We have a lot to talk about."

The child's breathing was already steady with slumber. With a final kiss to the top of her head, Lynnie headed downstairs to finish putting away the leftovers. She was in the kitchen when the doorbell rang.

"I'll get it," said Bethy. She returned a moment later, her face chalky white. In her arms she carried a pile of thorny weeds. Lynnie gave her an understanding look. She went to the china closet and chose a large vase. With a gentle nod to her sister, she took the thick bouquet of blooming roses from her sister's arms and tenderly arranged them.

Looking away from the thorny bouquet, Bethy spoke in a quiet voice, "Granny would have loved those roses, wouldn't she?"

Matthew Warner
SPRINGS ETERNAL

Besides books such as *The Organ Donor* and *Horror Isn't A 4-Letter Word*, MATTHEW WARNER is the proud papa of baby Owen, a sweet little boy possessing hypnotic powers over all who behold him. Matthew is married to webmistress and artist extraordinaire Deena Warner, and they live and work together in Staunton, Virginia, just a hop, skip, and a mountain range away from beautiful West Virginia. Come visit him at matthewwarner.com.

It only made sense that a former mineral springs resort in the middle of nowhere, West Virginia, came out of nowhere as you approached it. One moment, John Linden was winding his sedan down a valley of featureless farm lands in Monroe County, and the next, a hotel designed by none other than Thomas Jefferson was smack-dab in front of him.

Smack-dab. Yep, he better get used to phrases like that if he was going to fit in and land this job as a handyman. That, and *ain't*, *y'all*, and *fixin' to*. Whatever it took to put old man Lewis at ease.

The old man, hisownself (that was another one), emerged from between the Doric columns of the hotel's long porch and jogged across the lawn to him. Aside from hiking boots and a hunting cap with ear flaps—no doubt because it was colder than a witch's armpit this morning—Mr. Lewis looked about as stereotypically West Virginian as Donald Trump. He wore an expensive suit and tie and a prissy little moustache.

"John, my good sir. Most pleased you could make it. Welcome to Old Sweet Springs."

Didn't sound like a West Virginian, either. As John shook the offered hand—soft skin—he realized he would have to revise his assumptions about this area.

"Feeling's mutual, sir. So, is that the building I'll be working on?" He stopped himself from putting a twang on *workin'*. Maybe he could just be himself.

"Perhaps. But we're nearly done renovating the Jefferson building. When we reopen that as a resort—can you believe it's been ninety years?—I'm confident guests will luxuriate in splendor. They'll feel like all the U.S. presidents who have ever stayed here."

But John's attention was already wandering to the ruinous structure behind him. He couldn't help himself.

"Ah, yes," Mr. Lewis said. "I see you've already found your project."

"Sir?"

"That's the bathhouse. I can't very well reopen a mineral springs resort when its central attraction resembles the Parthenon after the siege of the Venentians, now can I?"

Mr. Lewis laughed at his own joke as he unlocked a tall metal gate so they could enter. He tossed the key to John. "You'll need this."

John smiled. This would be easier than he thought.

The bathhouse was little more than four vine-covered walls surrounding a pool floating with algae. A corner of it lay collapsed in a pile of bricks and wood as if God had smashed it in a fit. One end of the pool trickled away into an overflow ditch that John knew fed into Cove Creek.

Mr. Lewis peered into the pool's black depths. "Its appearance belies its wonder."

"Sir?"

"This spring. The Indians believed it could cure disease."

"I know."

"Oh, you do?"

"I—I mean—" He averted his gaze. "I mean I *heard* it was a historic spring."

"Indeed. Who knows, it may have been Ponce de Leon's Fountain of Youth!"

John nodded and tried to appear stoic. He leaned forward to find the pool's bottom but couldn't see it.

"Careful you don't fall in."

"Oh, don't worry, sir. I can't swim." And that was the truth.

"Ah."

Mr. Lewis suddenly appeared unsure of himself. Maybe it was time to get this charade firmly onto the road.

"So, sir, what do I need to get started?"

"Ah, well, let's go back to my office. After you sign some paperwork, we can continue your orientation."

John followed him back to the gravel service road. His gaze

swept over his surroundings as he contemplated the forthcoming tour of things he cared little about: the barren trees with the mountains in the distance, the dead grasses and weeds, the ancient hotel building with its windows staring out at him.

Just hold it together a little longer, he told himself. *The old man will be out of your hair soon.*

At Mr. Lewis's direction, he shut and locked the metal gate. The old man stared at John's wedding band. "I didn't know you were married. Is your wife here?"

With the gate locked, John turned to face him. He groped for his best stoic mask. "She'll be joining me shortly."

Luckily, a pick-up truck pulled up alongside them. A white-haired woman and a young man greeted them.

"Ah. John, let me introduce my family."

A false grin slipped into place as John made his pleasantries. Yes, sir, he sure was good at putting people at ease.

* * *

On the night John finally sneaked out to the bathhouse, it was no longer colder than a witch's armpit. It was worse, frostier than a witch's bosom on Christmas morning. He found he rather enjoyed fake-hick expressions like that, regardless that he seemed to be the only hick around here, fake or otherwise.

His breath steamed against the car's windshield as he drove up the service road. His headlights were off, but he saw just fine because he'd waited for the full moon. Its glow illuminated the well-worn copy of *The Legend of Ponce de Leon* on the passenger seat. He glanced at it before climbing out.

His hands trembled as he unlocked the big metal gate. This is why he'd bothered to apply for the job at all: to acquire the key. He parked inside the gate's perimeter, then returned to close it again.

At last, it was time. He opened the trunk.

Inside lay a black bodybag. He hoisted it in front of him and carried it to the edge of the pool. There, he opened it.

Emily.

It didn't matter how many times he saw it. The sight of his wife's remains always stabbed him in the heart. His lips trembled as he tried to hold it in. He imagined his eyes were like this place: an old sweet spring, ready to flow again.

The doctors had managed to extract the baby's body from her, but because the child was so premature, he hadn't dug it up like Emily. Once Emily was alive again, they would make more—wouldn't they?

But if this didn't work, he was through. One way or another, he vowed this would be the last night he endured life without his wife.

Emily still smelled like the formaldehyde they used to embalm her, but after a whole year, her body had still deteriorated. He thought he'd been good with her. He took so many pains to keep her dry and refrigerated. He touched her no more than necessary. But still, his wife now was just papery skin stretched tight over bone.

"It doesn't matter. I'll still love you."

Carefully, he lifted her from the bag and lowered her into the pool. His hands immediately went numb in the freezing water.

Gases no longer remained in Emily's body to keep her bouyant, so he stayed crouched by the pool, holding her afloat. A burning sensation replaced the numb feeling. He prayed, dear God, that it was water's magic at work and not just his blood solidifying in the cold.

Minutes ticked by. Emily's fragile, parchment-like skin began to slough away from her neck, revealing the hump of a vertebrae. A cloud of skin cells formed around her and floated toward the drainage ditch.

"No. Oh, God, no."

His tears dripped into the water.

"I tried. Emily, I tried. How can I go on without you?"

Reluctantly, he began hauling her out. But everything had gone clumsy in the cold. He lost his grip and dropped her into the water.

"No!"

His wife sank to the bottom like a stone. John sobbed as he lost sight of her. The only thing left of her was a growing cloud of deterioration on the surface. If he could swim, he would risk hypothermia to rescue her, but now it was hopeless.

The book lied to him. They were all liars. Old Sweet Spring couldn't bring the dead back to life. It wasn't the Fountain of Youth.

Screw it. He would jump in after her anyway. There was no point in going on.

The moon stared impassively as John stood up and spread his arms. He threw his head back and allowed himself to fall into the water.

The shock of cold momentarily robbed him of the ability to breathe, but when he regained it, he found he couldn't bring himself to inhale. The survival instinct was too strong. With his eyes pressed tightly shut, he slowly exhaled bubbles and allowed himself to sink. The freezing water poked icy fingers through his clothes and body.

When he could resist it no longer, he inhaled.

Water tasting of soil and stone filled his lungs—and he immediately coughed and choked. He spasmodically inhaled again, and he was drowning, oh God, he was drowning, and his arms and legs wouldn't obey his will, instead trying to swim to the surface as he inhaled again and choked some more. Bright lights appeared behind his eyes, and he lost consciousness.

Sometime later, he awoke on the bottom of the pool.

He was still numb. Water squished in his lungs. But he was alive.

The spring. It couldn't bring the dead back to life, as he'd hoped, but it could indefinitely sustain the living.

No. *No.*

It meant he would live without her. Forever.

Mark Justice
THE ANGRY DARK

MARK JUSTICE lives near the West Virginia border, where he hosts a morning radio show. His contributions have appeared in *The Book of Lists: Horror*, *The Horror Library Vol. 2* and *3* and in *Legends of the Mountain State Vol. 1* and *2*. His first collection, *Looking at the World With Broken Glass in My Eye*, will be published in 2010 by Graveside Tales. He blogs regularly at http://markjustice.blogspot.com/.

Was I born here? In Matewan?

No, but it seems like I've been here forever. I first saw this place in 1969, when the world was a very different place.

* * *

The town was so small. That was the first thing I noticed.

It was like a model of a town. A Hollywood movie set. Any minute now Andy Griffith would stroll out of the barbershop and walk to the courthouse, then the director would yell "Cut!" and the actors and crew would return to their real lives of mansions, limousines and fancy parties.

"Oh, wow," Heather said from the driver's seat. "This is nothing like Charlotte."

"I thought you'd been here before."

"Yeah, but I was just a little kid," she said.

On the radio, Bobby Goldsboro sang "Honey," which was, in my opinion. one of the worst songs of all time. Yet it seemed to play every fifteen minutes that year. It was giving me a headache. I snapped the radio off.

"Why'd you do that?" Heather said. "I love that song."

"Can we just stop somewhere? If I don't get out for a minute I'll throw up."

She laughed. "Pocahontas, you're such a drama queen."

I sighed. Pocahontas was Powhatan, and my grandmother was full blood Cherokee. But since I had told Heather this many times, I didn't bother to mention it again.

She steered the Volkswagen microbus toward a parking spot at the top of a hill on the town's main street. I climbed out of the cramped passenger compartment. The VW was a bucket of bolts that Heather had borrowed from another girl on our floor. I was surprised it got us this far.

Heather hopped out of the van. "Oh, wow," she said again.

The little town was bordered on one side by a river and by a mountain on the other. The street was lined by a few clean, brightly painted businesses. Directly across the street from us was the Matewan Motor Court.

A metallic groaning came from the VW.

"Crap," Heather said. It was the closest she came to swearing. "Forgot to set the brake." She slid back into the van and yanked on the emergency brake. When she exited the vehicle again she said, "Thanks for coming. Granny will be happy here. I can tell."

"Sure," I said. I didn't add that I wished more than anything that I'd stayed back at UNC, even if it meant my ex-boyfriend Richie would spend all weekend calling and dropping by with the idea of charming me into getting back together. The idea of a road trip was tempting yesterday. But now, standing in this tiny burg in the shadow of the mountain, I just wanted to get back.

"What now?" I said.

"We have to find the right spot. Come on." Heather crossed the empty street. I followed.

We entered the motel's office, accompanied by the ringing of a bell over the door. A large older man came out of a curtained back room, wiping his mouth with a checkered cloth. He had just a little white hair on the top of his head, and he peered at us through glasses parked on the end of his nose. He was dressed in blue jeans, suspenders and a white dress shirt that strained across his ample belly.

"Help ya?" he said.

"Hi. I'm Heather and this is my friend Pocahontas."

The man raised one eyebrow and studied me.

"It's actually Rachel," I said.

"You be needing a room?"

"What we really need," Heather said, "is information."

She was petite, cute and blonde, and most everyone was happy to speak with her, including the motel man. He stuck out a big hand.

"Heather, I'm Mack. What can I do for ya?"

I was tall and gangly, with a big nose and hair the color of coal, so I was used to Heather getting all the attention.

"I need to know where the massacre happened," Heather said.

"Ah," Mack said. "This might take a while, and my soup's getting cold. Why don't you come back here and join me? You too, Rachel."

We followed him through the parted curtains into a small kitchen. It was a clean room and smelled of fresh baked bread and spices. There was a big metal pot on the stove. One place was set at the table. There was a half-filled bowl of soup and a wooden cutting board with most of a loaf of bread. Mack opened a cabinet and removed two bowls and two glasses. From a drawer he produced a pair of spoons.

"We couldn't impose," I said.

"You're not. 'Sides, does it look like I could finish all that soup? Also, this is my ma's secret recipe, so if you don't eat you'll insult the memory of the meanest woman who ever lived in Mingo County." He laughed.

We sat at the table and Mack filled our bowls. Then he poured drinks from a big mason jar. "Sun tea," he said. "Made it this morning."

The vegetable soup and homemade bread were delicious. Compared to the food at the school cafeteria, this was a feast. Mack finished his soup, took a long drink of tea and cleared his throat.

"The massacre." he said. "I never understood why a quiet little town has produced so much violence. There was the nearby Hatfield-

McCoy feud in the 1880s. Then forty years later, the massacre."

"It was because the coal miners wanted to unionize wasn't it?" Heather said.

"Yes, ma'am. My daddy was one of the miners. They had to work in terrible conditions from dawn till dusk. The pay was terrible, and the companies treated these men worse than dogs."

"So why didn't they go find a job somewhere else?" I said.

"Jobs were scarce back then. Folks around here didn't go to college. You either farmed or worked in the mines. Eventually, the miners wanted to form a union. Once the mine company got wind of it, they brought in a bunch of union busters from an agency in Bluefield. Back then, the company owned everything—the mine, the stores, even the miners' houses. The thugs were brought in to throw the union organizers out of their homes."

"They could do that?" Heather's eyes were wide.

"They tried," Mack said. "But we had a good man for a sheriff, and he fought back. On May 19 he got a bunch of the miners together, and they met the union busters over at the train depot. Things got tense from the get-go. My daddy was there. He said nobody knew who shot first, but when it was over a lot of men were dead. A few of ours, but more of theirs."

Heather nodded. She had a far-away look on her face.

"Why are you two so interested in this dusty old piece of history?" Mack said. "You working on a school project?"

Heather shook her head. "One of those miners who died was my grandfather."

No one spoke for a moment. Then Mack asked Heather for the name of her grandfather. She told him.

"I remember him," Mack said. "Rather, I remember the name. I was just a squirt back then. In the days and years after, my daddy talked about him a lot. By all accounts, your grandad was a fine man."

"Why didn't you end up in the mines?" I said.

"I wanted to. And that led to the only real fight my daddy and I ever had. He hated the mines, and he didn't want me to have any part of it. He called the mine The Angry Dark. He made me promise I'd try something else before I went to the mine. So I joined the Navy, then tried college for a couple of years before I came home and opened this little place. It ain't much, but the day I opened the doors was the only time I ever saw my daddy cry." Mack turned his face way from us. He cleared his throat.

The sun was starting to go down, and I was getting restless. I touched Heather's arm. "I guess we need to do this."

She nodded, before turning back to Mack. "Thank you for your time and this fine food. Can I ask you for one more favor?"

"Sure," Mack said. "You want to pay your respects?"

Heather nodded. "That's part of it. My grandmother passed away last week."

"I'm truly sorry."

Heather smiled. "Thanks. She told me that when she was gone, she wanted her ashes scattered here in Matewan where my grandfather died. Can you show us the spot, Mack?"

He stood from the table. "Let's go before it gets dark."

* * *

After all these years I still don't know why Heather and I became friends. She was all light and happiness. I was the opposite. I suppose we bonded over our love of books and music. Also we had both been raised by our grandmothers. Mine told me stories about the *Yunwi Tsunsdi'*—the Little People—and The Raven Mocker, who robs the dying of their lives. Heather's granny told her about the hardscrabble life of a coal miner's wife and of the treachery and greed of the company. In our dorm room, Heather kept a photograph of her grandparents. Both were thin as rails, gazing at the camera with solemn expressions, the look of people who had seen what life offered them and found it to be bleak.

Our separate lives had brought us here together, where our destinies would forever be entwined.

We crossed the street to the microbus. Heather got in the front seat and searched through the trash in the back until she found what she was looking for. It was a small wooden box with a carving of a rose inlaid on its surface.

"I'm ready," she said.

Mack led us down the gradual slope of the main street. Near the end of the street, on the river side of the town, was the depot. The building was deep in shadows. The sunset dappled the sky with swaths of red and orange.

Mack stepped to the center of the street. There was no traffic.

"It happened here." His gesture encompassed both sides of the street. "I watched from up the hill. The battle seemed to go on for a long time, but it was really just a couple of minutes."

He grew silent. Heather bowed her head. The box containing her grandmother's ashes was clasped to her chest. When the sound came, I was the first to hear it.

It was a metallic rending, a harsh screech, followed by a loud thump. I turned toward the top of the hill and saw a larger patch of darkness roll toward us.

It was the microbus. The brakes or the transmission must have failed. Unable to move I watched the black shape speed closer

I heard Heather scream at the same instant she shoved me. I was thrown to the sidewalk and landed on my back. I saw the VW strike Heather. She was flung into the air. The microbus sped on, jumped the sidewalk and crashed into the front of the train depot. Heather struck the pavement, as crooked and unmoving as a broken doll. The box shattered on the street. Its contents drifted down like snow.

* * *

After talking to the police, Mack insisted I spend the night at the motel. I tried to sleep, but I kept hearing the sound of the impact. I eventually returned to the office where I found Mack standing at the window, staring outside. He held me as I cried. When the sun rose, he fixed us toast and eggs and then I made some calls. After noon, I returned to my room and slept until nightfall.

When I arose and showered, Mack had warmed up the soup. I told him I had to return to the depot before I left. He offered to go with me. I declined.

I made my way down the street. Again, the town seemed empty. I stood on the sidewalk very near the spot I had landed last night. In the dim glare from a distant streetlight I couldn't see the blood stain. I imagined Heather's blood seeping through the cracked surface of the street, joining with the blood of her grandfather and the other victims of the violence nearly a half century ago.

I started to cry again. "I'm sorry, Heather," I whispered.

I was sorry I wasn't a better friend. I was sorry I had lived while she didn't.

A harsh odor drifted across the darkness, a smell I didn't recognize. The night suddenly seemed very cold, as though the temperature had drooped twenty degrees in a single second.

The street gradually grew brighter, and in the center of the road I saw moving figures. There were several men, thin but solid. Their clothes and their faces were spotted with coal dust. They carried rifles and shotguns. One of the men in particular seemed familiar.

As they passed me, I saw another figure trailing close behind. She looked as sad and as tough as I recalled from the photograph, but now she also looked proud, a woman who had finally come home.

And bringing up the rear of the procession was a young woman. She stood straight and walked with determination just a few steps behind her grandparents.

As she passed me, Heather paused for a moment. She smiled, then continued on.

The glow faded, and I was left alone in the darkness.

* * *

That's how I ended up here. Oh, I went back to college and finished out the year. But I couldn't quit thinking about this place. So the next summer I came back. Mack gave me a job. I think he knew he was sick. After he passed, I took over the motel.

I'll never be rich. Of course, I never wanted that. I just wanted a life lived well, with good friends. I've found that in Matewan.

I must admit I go back to the depot every now and then, always at night. I've never seen Heather again or any of the rest. Sometimes I smell that acrid odor. I've learned that it's the distinctive stench of calcium carbide, the fuel for the lamps the old miners used. Its stink would get the devil's approval.

Still, I think I'll see Heather again. In this life or the next. I often wonder if she found her way to the light. I hope so. If anyone deserved it, it was her.

The other alternative is too horrible for me to contemplate. I can't think of anything worse than spending eternity in The Angry Dark.

Now run along. You've got your story, and I've got rooms to clean. But if you want to drop by later, I've got soup on. Then maybe we can stroll down to the depot.

Just for a minute.

JG Faherty
TRAPPED

JG FAHERTY is as Active Member in the Horror Writers Association, his credits include *Cemetery Dance Magazine*, www.WrongWorld.com, *Shroud Magazine*, *Doorways Magazine*, and several major anthologies. He also contributes columns, interviews, and book reviews to the HWA newsletter, *FearZone*, *Dark Scribe Magazine*, *Cemetery Dance*, and *Horror World*.

What does Hell sound like?

For me, it's a keening whistle, the demonic cry of a prehistoric metal beast approaching in the darkness. It's the sobbing of the dead, the screams of the tortured, and the thunderous, pounding roar of a thousand tons of steel appearing out of nowhere.

It is the sound of the iron beast hunting me in the permanent night of the tunnel, waiting for that moment when I'm just a footstep too slow, a stride too far from safety.

Odds are, it will get me. If it doesn't, one of the walking dead will. But I haven't given up hope. I only have to make it to morning. I will fight to the end, try my best to escape the Stygian passageway that holds me captive.

I don't want to die like the others.

* * *

The park ranger stared at us. "You folks made a wise decision visiting the ghost tunnel during the day, that's fer sure. Don't want to be in there at night."

He smiled, winked at the girls, and then climbed into his SUV. "Bad things go on in there at night." He waved at us and drove off.

Tanya turned to Jeff and me. "And you want to visit this Flinder-whatever place?"

"The Flinderation Tunnel," I said. "Don't listen to him, he was just pulling your leg. I've been in dozens of train tunnels, and I've never seen anything more dangerous than a spider."

It was true. Jeff and I had visited every haunted railroad station, trestle, and tunnel from New York to Ohio, all in the name of research for our book. The publishing company was paying us decent bucks, and we figured the least we could do in return was carry out a thorough investigation. So we'd decided to take the summer and visit all the places we'd read about, armed with camcorders and digital cameras.

Jeff put his arm around Stacy. We'd met her and Tanya a week earlier, and they'd decided to accompany us on a few of our ghost hunts. "Seriously. These places are all the same. Pop in, take some pictures, and then head to the nearest bar."

"Fine," Tanya said, looping her arm through mine. "Let's get this over with so we can have some real fun."

* * *

After a long drive, a short hike, and a walk down the abandoned railroad tracks, our arrival at the Flinderation Tunnel was anticlimactic. No strange voices called out to us, no ghostly figures waited to lure us in.

"This is it?" Stacy asked, staring at the dark hole.

"Told you," Jeff said. "No big deal." He took out his camcorder and started filming, while I snapped pictures of the entrance. Then we stepped inside.

The moment we entered the tunnel, something changed. The temperature dropped twenty degrees, the early afternoon light seemed hard-pressed to penetrate past the entrance, and a wild, hostile odor assaulted our noses.

Beneath all that was something worse, something that wrapped cold fingers around my bones and filled my stomach with razor-sharp ice. It took me a moment to recognize the feeling.

Fear.

"Jesus, this place stinks!" Jeff covered his nose and mouth with his free hand.

Hands grabbed me. "Rick, I don't like this. Can we go now?" In the near dark, Tanya's face was a pale moon, her eyes two black craters.

I was all set to say yes, when I noticed something in the light from Jeff's camcorder.

"Jeff, do you see that graffiti?"

"Yeah, wicked, isn't it?" He seemed unaffected by the dread that had my hands trembling.

The strange drawings on the brick walls were more than wicked; they were possibly the strangest things I'd ever seen. No phone numbers, no lovers' names, no gang symbols.

Just faces: screaming, terrified faces. I flicked on my flashlight and approached one. Rather than painted on, the images seemed burned right into the old brickwork. I waved my flashlight down both sides of the tunnel.

They were everywhere.

"The old pictures we looked at never had any graffiti in them," Jeff said, coming up next to me.

"Yeah." I didn't know what else to say. Something about those faces had me frozen in place. I couldn't look away.

I was still staring when Stacy spoke up. "Guys, I don't feel so good. I think I'm gonna be sick."

"All right, let's head back to the car and we'll. . ."

Something about the way Jeff's voice trailed away made me turn around. One look over my shoulder showed me what the problem was.

The circle of light marking the tunnel's entrance was gone.

"Everyone come here," I said, wondering just how long we'd been standing there. How could night have fallen without us noticing? "Grab hands and we'll follow the tracks out." At that point, I was only worried about someone tripping on the tracks and getting hurt in the dark.

Gravel and cinders crunched underfoot as I stepped forward, using my flashlight to guide us. I was so intent on our path I never noticed the figure in front of us until it spoke.

"They're commming."

My heart slammed into my ribs, and I jumped back a step. Behind me, one of the girls let out a small yelp and Jeff cursed. A scream of my own rose in my throat and stuck there as I brought the flashlight up, illuminating the source of the gruff voice.

His body dangled from the top of the opening, swaying back and forth at the end of the rope looped around his neck. His head hung to one side, the eyes wide and staring at us, two white orbs against his dark skin. His clothes were torn to shreds, and even in the shaky beam of my flashlight I could see the red welts covering his body.

He raised a hand and pointed at us. His mouth fell open, exposing a swollen tongue. *"Ruuun."*

That was when my scream finally escaped.

We turned and ran deeper into the tunnel, no longer holding hands, everyone shouting and cursing at once. Tanya fell. She cried out in pain, but I didn't bother asking if she was all right. I just grabbed her arm, hauled her up, and forced her to keep running. I tried aiming my flashlight forward, but between my arm moving and the two people in front of me, it did little to illuminate anything.

Then we heard it.

A long, mournful whistle, a sound that should have evoked nostalgic, sepia-toned memories, but instead froze my blood and set my stomach churning.

A train was coming.

"What the—" Jeff stopped running and the rest of us had to

swerve to the sides so we wouldn't crash into him. "This track is supposed to be abandoned."

"It's the ghost train," someone said. It took me a moment to realize it was me.

"Yeah right," Jeff said, turning to face me. Before he could go on, the whistle sounded again, coming from the direction we'd been running towards. This time I heard something else in it, something hidden beneath the somber howl: the terrible wailing of a thousand tortured souls crying out their pain and anguish.

"We gotta go back," I said. Stacy moaned, her face as white as winter ice.

Tanya clutched my arm. "That, that *thing* is back there."

A bright light appeared behind Jeff, giving me no chance to respond. At the same time, a sudden vibration ran through the tracks, shaking us where we stood.

"Hurry! We have to find one of the cubbys!" Clutching Tanya's hand, I ran back the way we'd come, only this time I kept the flashlight aimed at the side of the tunnel. I was searching for a cubbyhole, one of the safety areas the workers would have carved out so they could get away from the tracks when a train came through.

Behind us, the light grew brighter and the vibrations stronger. A thunderous noise filled the tunnel as tons of iron and steel bore down on us. The whistle sounded again, its deadly call so loud it seemed the engine was mere steps behind us. My guts convulsed and warm, sticky fluids ran down the backs of my legs, but I didn't slow down.

Three more steps and my flashlight revealed what I'd been praying for. A cubbyhole, only yards ahead and deep enough for all of us to fit in. I ran faster, pulling Tanya with all my might. As soon as I reached the cubby, I dragged her inside and turned to light the way for Jeff and Tracy.

Only they weren't there.

I cast the light further down the tunnel, spotted them a dozen paces back. Stacy was on her knees and Jeff was desperately trying to pull her up.

"Stacy!" Tanya jumped past me and ran back to her friend.

"Tanya! No!"

Everything happened so fast after that. The train, a bellowing, steaming behemoth whose cowcatcher glowed lava-red, barreled into them. For the briefest instant I saw the three of them frozen in time and space, their bodies rendered translucent, skeletons clearly visible, as if the train's headlamp was the world's most powerful x-ray machine.

Then they were gone and train was heading directly at me. I dove back into the cubby, pressed my back against the cold, slimy wall.

The train roared past, its details blurred from speed and the billows of scalding steam surrounding it. But some of the cars had windows, and in them I saw the source of the whistle's tormented cries.

Faces, dozens of them, all stretched into hideous masks of pain, mouths opened in unending screams. I closed my eyes before the last cars went by, unable to look at the agonized expressions any longer.

But not before I saw Jeff, Tracy, and Tanya in one of the windows, their once-happy faces already molded into tortured caricatures of humanity.

Hot winds pummeled me and tiny meteors of gravel and sand burned my exposed flesh. The bestial din of steel-on-steel seemed to go on forever.

Then it was gone.

I stayed on the ground, my body curled in a fetal position, until I was sure it wasn't coming back. Then I slowly sat up. I felt around with my hands until locating my flashlight; a couple of shakes and it came on. The light made me feel a little better, but it still took a while before I felt confident my legs would support me. When I finally did stand, I crept to the edge of the cubby and looked in both directions.

"It'll be back for you."

I stumbled away from the voice, tripped over a railroad tie, landed hard. Bringing the flashlight up, I shined it into the cubby.

A man in torn work clothes stood there, his head in his hands, his neck a ragged, bleeding stump.

"There's no escape. It'll keep comin' back 'til it gets ya."

I jumped to my feet and ran. The thing's laughter followed me, until another sound drowned it out.

The sound of the ghost train returning.

Once more I sprinted down the tracks until I found another

cubby. Once more I pressed myself against the crumbling bricks, only this time I kept my face turned away from the hellish locomotive, and my hands pressed tight over my ears.

* * *

Since then the train has gone by twice more. I don't know where the next cubbyhole is, or even if there is one. So I haven't moved, except when I use the flashlight to check for ghosts. I haven't seen any more of them, but I know they're out there.

I can hear them.

They laugh and argue and call for help. The hanged man, the headless rail worker, and who knows how many others. Sometimes I hear things moving, scratching. Gravel and cinders grinding under stealthy feet. But when I look, nothing's there.

I haven't given up hope, though. As long as nothing chases me from my hiding place, I can wait right here. Just a few hours; just until morning.

I will not die like the others.

I give my flashlight another shake. The bulb is sputtering, growing dimmer.

The sounds are getting closer.

And the laughter is getting louder.

VISIT
www.woodlandpress.com
for more information on your favorite
Woodland Press authors and book titles

118 Woodland Drive, Suite 1101
Chapmanville, WV 25508

Email: woodlandpressllc@mac.com

Cover artwork by graphic illustrator Julia Starr, of Brigham City, Utah.
You can find more of her work at night-fate.deviantart.com

© Copyright 2009. Each of the contributors to Legends of the Mountain State 3 own the individual copyrights to his or her work, but each has given Woodland Press certain literary rights making it possible to assemble their writings, along with others, in this historic title.